LIBERTY 2041

episode 2

Conceived & Written By
Carolyn & Robert Gold

2021

Series Summary: As an authoritative regime takes over the Earth to halt the rapid advancement of teens, an uprising occurs to repair the world.

Episode Summary:

The world is in crisis. Superhumans are experiencing life without computer enhancements. During a transformational event, they enter a new realm of awareness. Training to repair the world begins.

Distribution by KDP- Amazon and Ingram Spark

Title: Liberty 2041 Names: Carolyn Gold and Robert Gold - authors

thegoldtouch.net & liberty2041.com

ISBN: 978-1-952998-02-7 (print)

ISBN: 978-1-952998-03-4 (e-book)

[1. Computers— Fiction 2. Nanotechnology— Fiction 3. Expansive Intelligence— Fiction 4. Intellitela and Glåsse (devices)— Fiction 5. Scarsdale, N.Y. (Town)— Fiction]

Editor: Tuesday Thompson

Typesetter: Brent Meske

Publisher: The Gold Touch

INTRODUCTION

As very private people, unused to speaking about themselves, the authors are doing just that, through the pages of a series of futuristic novellas. Before meeting, Robert and Carolyn were fascinated by human behavior and sensory perceptions. As a result, they each developed professions that focus on how we function in the world and what can be done to improve it and benefit both children and adults.

In 2014, Robert was inspired to write a novel and came up with a lengthy manuscript for Liberty 2041. The storyline revolved around exceptional kids, the future of computer augmentation and a protagonist's predestined mission to repair the world. Four years later, once Carolyn entered the picture, it was clear they were brought together for many reasons, one being the development of this unique concept so it could be brought to light.

They formulated a way to divide the original single book concept into a series of episodic novellas. The original characters had already been created by Robert. Now ones were dreamed up by Carolyn to add substance to the storyline, allowing one to delve into rich emotional and physical landscapes.

The curtain is pulled back to reveal what hides behind the public persona and what molds their place in the world.

The series is meant to provide entertainment and a

healthy escape, but also to provide learning and teaching opportunities. The authors consider this series of episodic novellas a valuable tool with which to open a myriad of conversations on a variety of subjects, with people of all ages.

The Gold's philosophy is one where children are heard and respected, never judged nor labeled. The stories are meant to reassure the reader that uniqueness is indeed a gift unto itself, one to be nurtured and treasured.

They are a means of discovery by which one's fondest dreams, greatest fears, likes, dislikes, and failures, may very well lead to triumphs.

The authors' fondest wish is to inspire and motivate readers to accomplish things never thought possible.

To children of all ages…

May you always retain your sense of wonder.

May you find ways to nurture your soul.

May you find daily reasons to smile.

May you live bathed in light.

We thank every child and adult in our lives.

Our interactions inspire us to envision

a future filled with hope and possibility.

Carolyn & Robert Gold

TABLE OF CONTENTS

FLOWERS
ACT V

Speaking to thousands of spectators at the Jarvis Center was so exciting, and now— here I am, in a state of panic. Reporters are closing in on me. The crowd is roaring. I can't stand this a second longer. I scan the room for an escape route and locate the exit leading to the side of the building.

"Sorry, Mom but I'm outta here!"

"What, honey? I can't hear you very well," Mom shouts out.

"I said— I'm getting out of here!" I scream.

There're people waiting in line to congratulate me, but I dodge them like flags on a slalom. I push on the heavy, fire escape door and dash down the long corridor. My heart is pumping hard as tears stream down my face. What if someone's chasing me? I'm too scared to look over my shoulder to find out.

The last set of doors takes me to the street. I'm greeted by a blast of cold air. I wrap around to the front of the building and spot a car with an open door. The woman driver is waving at me.

I walk towards her… "Ouch!" Someone grabbed my left forearm really hard. It feels like my bones are rubbing together.

"Heeeey!" I yell at the woman with crazed, loopy eyes. "Let go of me, lady!" If there's one thing I hate more than noisy, crowded spaces, it's being grabbed by strangers in noisy, crowded places.

She fakes a smile and replies, "Jessica… it's me, Phaedra Aetós! You promised I'd have the exclusive if you won tonight's debate. Remember?"

"I've never seen you in my life! Reporters are all a bunch of manipulative liars and provocateurs! Let gooo!" I yell, feeling a blast on my face, but it's not cold air. I'm shoved into the car and huddle on the floor behind the driver's seat, in a fetal position. I hear myself sobbing hysterically. The driver jumps in and peers over from the front seat. "My word! Are you injured? How's your left arm?"

How can she be so focused on me when a herd of angry screaming beasts are banging on the car? The paparazzi are relentless.

A man's voice yells out, "Jessica, why are you hiding? Is it because you attacked Phaedra Aetós in public, and now you're ashamed?" Another says, "What's your friend Senator Kravitz going to think of you now, Little Miss

Self-righteous?" The final blow was, "You're just like the rest of the Hybrids… you're all just plain bat crazy!"

"Noooo, stop saying that, bunch of liars, all of you!" I yell back.

The driver interrupts, "Only one passenger?"

"What? Yes— No!" I snap. "My parents— they'll figure it out. Please! Get me out of here— now!"

The driver starts honking and accelerating with the brakes on, in hopes that the lunatics will disperse. I hear a siren. "Oh, no— not the police! Now I'm in real trouble. Please— help me!"

"You're safe, don't worry. Hold on tight— here we go!" The car screeches into traffic, full speed ahead.

The driver makes a sharp turn. "Ow-ow-ow— my arm!" I cry out.

"Sorry, I'm having to take a detour— we're being followed."

"What? By whom?"

"No idea, Miss… ?"

"Jessica— Jessica Stafford," I snap.

"Miss Jessica, hang in there, this may take a bit longer, we're taking back roads to get to the closest emergency clinic. Your arm could be dislocated, fractured— or worse."

"Whaaat?"

"Touch your face, how are your teeth? Anything bleeding, broken or chipped?"

"Why? What happened to me?"

"Do as I ask. I'll explain later."

I touch my face. It's wet, sticky, it hurts. Ugh… I can taste a little bit of blood inside my mouth.

"Painful cheek and jaw, no broken teeth…" I report then start hyperventilating. "No clinic… take me… home… my parents… must be… really worried… they'll fix me…"

The driver tosses over a brown paper bag with food in it. "I'm bleeding— not hungry," I scream.

"Take the food out and breathe into the bag!" she instructs. "I've alerted your parents; they'll meet us at the clinic. While we're there, someone will be taking your statement."

The brown bag helps me breathe and speak, "No more statements to the press— I'm talked out!" I try stretching my legs out, one at a time and lean my head against the car door.

"Not to the press, to the authorities to press charges. That lunatic woman that came at you is guilty of assaulting a minor. She's been taken into custody. You had plenty of credible witnesses."

"Assaulted… Outside the Jarvis?" I squeal.

"Yes, child, calm down. Listen to what I have to say— listen. My name is Amana. Have you ever heard that name before?"

"No… I haven't," I say, sobbing again.

"In Swahili it means warrior at heart, loyal, faithful. I was born in Tanzania, East Africa. It's near the ocean. Do you like the ocean?"

I hear myself exhale, "Yes…"

"Imagine… The Good Lord placed me there one day and the next, he decided to move me across the world. It must have been so I could be right here with you— right now."

"Whaaat?"

"You remember seeing me outside, a woman all dressed up in a bright floral dress, waving enthusiastically, outside the Jarvis."

"Yes… I remember, but I didn't notice your dress— sorry."

"Want to hear something really funny? I wasn't waving at you. I was waving at my friend; we were on our way to a celebration. You jumped in my car instead of her."

"Ohhh nooo… I'm sooo sorry… We need to go back!" I remark frantically.

"She's fine. I'm sure she went on without me. Things like this always happen to me."

"What do you mean?"

"Let's just say it was no coincidence, that you chose a paramedic as the driver for your getaway car," she chuckles.

"Thank you… so much… What were you celebrating?"

She hesitates. "Oh… nothing special… just my engagement."

My loud sobs resemble Niagara Falls. My eyes are swelling and getting tight.

"Don't worry about it. Everyone will have a good laugh. It's not the first time I've missed an event. We'll have another chance to get together next week, at the wedding," she reassures me with her rich, melodic accent.

I reach for the brown bag again to stop hyperventilating. "Thank you, Amana. You literally… saved my life. Does this… make you an angel?"

"That's funny… my fiancée says the same thing. I think of myself as a messenger who listens, then all I have to do is do my job."

Since I can't see Amana, I decide to visualize her wearing a beautiful, emerald green turban. That's what must make her so balanced. How else could she be able to soothe a hysterical, injured teen, scrunched in her back seat. I touch my left arm with my right hand yell out, "Nooo, pleeease!"

"What's wrong, child?"

"The very grown-up, pale pink, silk blouse my best friend lent me for good luck is torn to shreds. It's ruined— forever!"

The sound of Caribbean metal drums starts playing in the background, reducing my wardrobe malfunction anxiety. I rest my eyes and imagine soft, tropical breezes blowing on flowers and leaves.

Two clink sounds come from the Glåsse on the back of Amana's seat. I automatically use my left hand to push myself away to see who's on the screen. I yell out in pain, it's excruciating. This is beyond horrible, terrible; pain and anxiety levels are escalating. How am I going to function without the use of my dominant hand ever again? Being a lefty is challenging enough. Through my very swollen eyes, I can make out that someone's waving. "Jessica Stafford… hi!"

This must be a pain hallucination, but I'll ask anyway, "Who is this— really?"

"It's me— really, I'll prove it." A familiar, gentle voice hums a few bars of a song and then says, "Sorry to intrude, but I had to— I just saw what happened and wanted to reach out and offer you my support."

"You whaaat…?"

"Are you alright?"

"I'm not really sure… a driver is taking me to a clinic."

"Oh, my stars! May I keep you company till you get there, then?"

I grunt back.

"I'm one of your biggest fans, Jessica. Your performance tonight, at the debate, was phenomenal. I was on the edge of my seat the whole, entire time. As they said on the news, you're a force to be reckoned with!"

My arm is throbbing and beyond excruciating.

She adds, "Once this blows over… would you consider… I'd really love it if… Could we collaborate…?"

"Collaborate? Us?… How… Why?"

"Think about it, we have lots in common. We're both teenaged girls, compelled to speak our minds and motivate others. We both want to change the world. You do it by debating; I do it by composing."

"Wow… I never thought…" I whisper.

"It's never been my goal to be famous, and I have a feeling it's the same for you. But, either way, as of tonight, you are famous, so I want to be the first to welcome you to the RCC."

"To the whaaat?"

"It's short for Reluctant Celebrity Club!" I try to giggle but moan in more pain instead.

"How're you doing back there, Miss Jessica?" Amana inquires.

"I'm talking to… a new friend."

"How very lovely," Amana replies with a smile in her voice.

My new friend continues, "It gets rather lonely at the top of this mountain called Fame. So if you ever need to talk, just reach out. Okay?"

"I will… thank you…" I reply as if that was a normal conversation. But nothing about today has been normal. I just spoke to Sahrit Bana, the most famous teen singer-songwriter on Earth!

"Jessica, we're here now," Amana announces.

"I can't move, I'm wedged in." I yell out in a panic. Amana encourages me to remain calm while I'm placed on a gurney.

"Miss Jessica…? Can you hear me…?" I recognize the voice and open my eyes. There's my angel's face for the first time. She isn't wearing an elegant, green turban like I'd imagined, but she is very regal looking.

She's smiling and reassuring my poor worried parents as I'm coming out of anesthesia. I can't say much, but do point at something sparkly around her neck. She touches the beautiful pendant and says, "This is tanzanite. It comes from my home country." She takes it off and places it in my right hand, gold chain and all. "This is for you, Miss Jessica Stafford. You are a very brave warrior and a messenger. Be sure to listen carefully and do your work."

Sunday, March 3, 2041 7:00 PM

I hear a voice saying, "*Hola dormilona*, sleepy head, time to waaake uuup…"

"Sari… oh… wow… you came to see me at the clinic?"

"Clinic? You're at home, in your bed, silly girl."

"Ohhh… Thanks for waking me up. I was having that recurring dream of 'The Incident' from last year. It was so awful at first, but this time, the scene went on to when we first met."

"Groovy! Hope my performance was award worthy," she giggles.

"Yes, definitely! I owe you big time," I reply as I sit up, trying to wrangle my wild hair.

"D'you have a sec?" Sahrit asks.

I glance at the time. "Just about— I have a meeting in a few."

"Got it, me too. I need to ask for a humongous favor. It has to do with my concert this coming weekend in New York."

Ooops! Glad she mentioned it, I had forgotten all about it. Thanks a lot— Mr. Chancellor!

"Do you need help filling some empty seats in the arena?" I reply awkwardly.

Bleep!

Rude.

Hope I didn't hurt her feelings by covering up my forgetfulness.

Chimes…

"If anything, we're oversold. People are on standby to get in. Can you believe it? Anyway, I was wondering… if… umm… Gosh, you know how hard it is for me to ask for stuff."

"Just spit it out. How bad could it be? How do you entertain thousands and stay so shy?"

"Hard to explain, really, when I'm around music… it's like I'm in another dimension."

"Sounds really cool, wish I could escape from reality like that."

"Speaking of escaping… that's what I wanted to ask you about. Could I hide out at the Stafford Inn? I really don't want to stay at a big busy multiplex. My entourage insists on wanting to try some new fancy hotel in the city.

I feel 'peopled out' just thinking about it. If I could chill out in a quiet, normal place before and after the show, I'd offer a much better performance. Yes? Maybe?"

"Sounds perfectly perfect to me, not sure about the normal, quiet part, though," I reply, half joking. "Things have been rather dramatic since Jake the Jock was arrested and jailed for rioting."

"Oh, my stars… I thought things had calmed down. If it's not a good time, I can always climb up a tree in Central Park and camp out. It'll be groovy to practice songs with the birds. No one will even know I'm there. So, just in case the Inn is not available, I'll pack light."

"Silly bird… you always have a way of making me laugh."

"I wasn't kidding, I really do know how to pack light!"

"I'll let you know. Ciao for now, Flower Child."

A giant peace sign designed with fresh flowers as they open to full blooms, takes over my entire Glässe. The background becomes gradually darker, the blooms close up. The screen goes back to normal. Wow! Gorgeous! Oops! I barely have enough time to get ready for what could be the most important meeting of my entire life! Flower Power starts playing; my spheres love dancing to it.

"Thank you, Intelly," I whisper. "No matter what people say, you take good care of me." I get up, splash cold water on my face and come back to bed. Better do some body brushing to get rid of all the bad body sensations left over from that nightmare.

Ahh… much better… Now— what shall I wear? Instead of bothering Jazz, I'll attempt to channel her. She'd probably say that based on my multifaceted personality, the outfit should be comfortable so that I can remain calm and feel confident. I pull open the old dresser's bottom drawer. Wait— what's this package nestled among my things? It's wrapped in pale pink tissue and held together by a matching ribbon with tiny pearls on it. When did Jazz manage to sneak this in? This super soft, long sleeved blue-green turtleneck matches the color of my walls perfectly. The design on the fleece lined leggings looks like partially colored in floral patterns. As I pick them up a handwritten note falls on the floor.

> Discover the pleasure of expressing your softer side. Try the feeling on for size.
> Love, Mademoiselle Rossé.

As I put on my new top, I wonder if the pain in my arm will ever go away. Why do I need this constant reminder? A puff of eucalyptus comes to the rescue, helping me exhale. "I'm so ready to move on," I say out loud. I decide to make myself a high ponytail, tilting my head towards the right. I use the ribbon as a headband to exercise my feminine creativity. Standing in front of the mirror, I proclaim, "Today you'll express your softer side." I blow myself a little kiss and wink.

With a few minutes to spare, there's just enough time to prop up pillows just the way I like them. Two under my left arm for support, one under each knee and the rest for my back. The timer on the Glåsse indicates it's 7:27:00 PM. Jazz, Tomas, Josef and Stefan appear.

"Hey everyone, thanks for being here— ahead of schedule!" We exchange comments, except for Tomas, who looks just like he did earlier on my wall— highly preoccupied.

"Is anyone else coming to our meeting?" I'm compelled to ask. Tomas ignores my question because at exactly 7:30:00 PM his friend shows up on the screen.

"Good evening everyone, my name is Dahvid Toledano. It is a pleasure to be here."

"Good evening, Dahvid," I respond, "how do you spell that?"

"D-a-h-v-i-d." He smiles in acknowledgement, but his eyes are darting back and forth on his screen. Looks like he's searching for something of great importance.

"Tomas, did you have a chance to get that additional information we needed from Ms. Stafford?" he asks. Tomas looks down at his own screen, shaking his head and typing frantically.

The meeting hasn't even begun, and I can already feel my temper rising. "Dahvid… what are you referring to? Maybe, if you had asked me, you'd already have the answer," I snap.

Bleep!

Rude.

His response is overly polite, especially for someone our age. "Certainly, Ms. Stafford. I have extensive data on the Tallon-Saldane brothers, but I do not have much on Ms. Jasmin Ross. So before we proceed, can you tell me, briefly, why you have chosen her to be part of this meeting?"

Guess I should be grateful that he's so thorough, questioning everyone's credibility. Why didn't Tomas provide him with this before the meeting? My screen's already turning orangey-red so I take a deep breath and respond, "It's hard to be brief when it comes to Jazz, I mean, Ms. Ross. There's so much to her personality, she's multidimensional." I pause to gather my thoughts. "We've been neighbors and best friends our entire lives. We work incredibly well together. She's highly intuitive. I trust her input 100% of the time. She is an administrative and tech wizard. It's safe to say she's indispensable. I don't know what I'd do without her in my life."

Stefan gives my comments thumbs up. Jazz smiles, wiping away happy tears.

"Thank you for that very clear picture. Tomas also speaks very highly of Ms. Ross."

"So why did you need to hear it from me?"

Bleep!

Patience.

"For several reasons, one of which includes capturing a statement directly from you for our voice recognition system."

"Why are you using voice recognition on me? Wish you had mentioned that beforehand. There are laws— you know?"

Grrr… I feel so paranoid all of a sudden.

Bleep!

Trust.

Dahvid smiles calmly, "If you recall, Ms. Stafford, you and your group are within our secure system already, we refer to it as Tower.

Some of the modalities can be accessed by speaking or, in some cases, by singing."

"So Dahvid, tell us about yourself? Jessica and I tried meeting with you earlier, but…" Josef says as Tomas straightens up in his seat, looking away, anticipating confrontation.

"My sincere apologies. As you can well imagine, today has been an exceptionally busy day around the globe. In the future, we will make sure to have things set up ahead of time so that our meetings run efficiently."

How elegant, Dahvid directed his comments at no one in particular. I need to do that.

Chimes…

Wait— did he say future meetings? That's a little presumptuous on his part. Why would we meet again?

Bleep!

Patience.

A vid screen pops open on my Glåsse. Sahrit is playing the piano and singing. Her accompanist, on the guitar has his back to the camera, until he turns and smiles at whomever is filming. The caption says, "Groovin' at Inspiration Station with my friend, collaborator and producer, Dahvid."

"Do you happen to know Sahrit Bana?" I ask

without missing a beat.

"I would expect everybody knows her. She's an international star," he responds with surprise in his voice.

I smile awkwardly, I have no comeback. Glad Sahrit knows him so well.

Chimes…

Dahvid continues, "Back to my credentials, Tomas and I connected on a tech platform for like-minded people."

"What's the platform?" I ask presumptuously, expecting to hear him say Liberty World.

"Segovia is a platform for young people from eight to eighteen who are techies and accomplished musicians."

"Do you have to audition to enter the group?" I inquire, wanting to hide my true motives.

Dahvid responds, "Music is a universal form of communication. It becomes apparent, rather quickly, if members are fluent in that language— or not."

I'm trying to imagine what instrument Tomas could possibly be good at.

Bleep!

Judgmental.

Jazz chimes in, "From what I know, Segovia is

a pretty exclusive group! I'm so proud of you, Tomas! Congratulations!"

Tomas blushes, producing a crooked little smile.

Dahvid continues, "My parents have lived in many places. I was born in NYC and then moved to Dallas, where my brother and sister were born. I am involved with businesses and tech, speak several romance languages: Spanish, French…"

I interrupt, to prove I'm listening, "Did you know that Jazz speaks fluent French!"

"*Magnifique!* " He responds with a playful grin. Jazz giggles with delight as Stefan frowns.

Tomas jumps in, "Can we pleeease skip the international pleasantries and get on with the meeting? I've prepared an introduction."

"Fine— let's move on," I reply flatly.

Tomas clearers his throat and begins, "We're all aware that our current situation is dire. Things have got to change quickly, or we'll be in serious trouble. Dahvid has joined us tonight because time is of the essence. He and his tech group can be instrumental in assisting by making changes in the world by manipulating time."

Dahvid takes a sip of something from a sparkly, iridescent, turquoise thermos. He seems a bit nervous. "Thank you for that introduction, Tomas. I appreciated the clever play on words."

Tomas gives him that same shy smile.

"My friend is referring to the team of dynamic tech designers and coders I associate with. Together, we are able to furnish specialized services in a short amount of time."

"What type of services do you offer, and why do you think we need any of them?" I ask abruptly.

Bleep!

Patience.

"Ms. Stafford, we have been following the content of your debates closely, and I'm a member of Liberty World. We are quite familiar with what is of vital importance to you," he responds with a polite but firm tone.

"*Touché,*" Tomas mumbles.

Dahvid continues. "Furthermore, to prove we are such a good fit, the top two department heads have offered to adapt their work schedules to align with yours."

"I thought techies work all hours," Stefan jabs to show off.

Dahvid explains that for us, they'd need to be available in real time but was not at liberty to get into specifics.

"Can you at least tell us their names?" I ask.

"Yes… Leonardo and Jordan."

"Both guys?" I ask sarcastically, "you should try having girls on your team for a change— we can be quite dynamic."

Bleep!

Back off.

My tone was a bit heavy-handed for a newcomer. Being playful and using the right tone are not my strong suits.

Chimes…

Dahvid clears his throat nervously, "Perhaps, if you would allow me to continue…?"

Instead of apologizing, I mimic zipping my mouth. He tries to contain his smile, "Jordan's discovery has led towards phenomenal advances. We are now able to extend human life for undetermined amounts of time."

"That's really fascinating… but isn't that outside the laws of nature?" Stefan inquires, sounding both curious and uncomfortable.

"Be assured that our work is exclusively science based. What was once considered to be outside the possibilities of nature is no longer the case, thanks to this breakthrough."

We learn that this can be done by applying a series of drops which are practical, portable, and can be made available at a moment's notice. Tomas interjects by explaining that these drops can develop new crystalline lenses in our eyes. "It's simple, metabolism and movement are altered, slowing down the flow of light. It's all about perception. As time accelerates, the world appears to slow down."

"Thank you for that, Tomas." Dahvid handles the takeover graciously. "To expand, the speed of light travels at one hundred, eighty-six thousand, two hundred eighty-two miles per second. This tech has the ability to slow time down further, to one hundred thousandths of the speed of light."

"Wait— that's only ten times faster than the speed of sound!" I exclaim.

Dahvid smiles, "Tomas, you were right, Ms. Stafford is quite brilliant and clearly a fellow Einstein *aficionada!* "

"Yes… and yes," Tomas agrees as his beyond-pale complexion, turns rosy pink. Even though he's facing down, his eyes are on me. Now— that's a first!

Dahvid takes another sip from his thermos and shares, "Let me present it differently… Imagine having the capacity to control time."

"Explain," Josef requests skeptically.

"For example, while you are accomplishing

certain tasks, those around you would appear to be in a frozen state. You would be operating at accelerated speeds."

"That— is— phenomenal!" Stefan exclaims.

"Yes, it is. Would you like to expand on this?" Dahvid asks.

Tomas clears his throat and announces, "What would normally take a year to accomplish, would take you nine hours."

"Why are you sharing this with us? Wait— I think I figured it out! Would this have anything at all to do with teaming up to infiltrate The World Chancellor's empire?" I'm feeling certain of the answer.

"Yes, exactly! Together, our groups would be quite powerful," Dahvid replies.

Before I can say anything else, Tomas breaks in, "Tell them about the other ideas!"

"Yes, of course. Leonardo has contributed towards developing interfaces that can assist in regaining control after our implants are disabled. There is a considerable learning curve to become proficient, but well worth the effort."

Stefan adds, "The military applications could be endless!"

"Josef, do you have comments or questions?" I

prompt.

"Are you implying you'd be willing to provide us with all of this technology?"

Dahvid nods and Stefan jumps in, "Why are you willing to give us so much power? What makes you so sure we wouldn't misuse it?"

"Your questions are excellent," Dahvid responds as he sips a couple more times.

What in the world is in that thermos? It's so distracting, especially when the shimmery bits catch the light.

Dahvid responds, "The idea of misuse or abuse has terrified our team, especially Leonardo. It was our friend, Tomas Kesher here, who reassured me that you, as a group, would handle it responsibly and appropriately. Leonardo had one condition."

"What condition was that?" I snap.

"In order to share our tech with you, we had to investigate your backgrounds."

"Whaaat? You dug into my private life?"

Bleep!

Your life is public record.

Grrr... My volcanic mood is bubbling up to the surface, turning my screen orangey-red. How can I cover it up? I inhale deeply and say, "I'm positive you found Stefan and Josef to be outstanding individuals having spotless reputations. I'm also positive that there'd be no reason to investigate my life… or Jazz's, for that matter, since we're not in the military."

Bleep!

Selfishness masked as concern.

It's official— I've lost my weak attempt at remaining cool tonight. I exhale as I lean back, defeated by my own emotions. This time, Dahvid doesn't take a small sip but two huge gulps of his magic potion. He clears his throat and adjusts the collar of his shirt. The color reminds me of the most perfectly perfect, spring morning sky.

Bleep!

Focus.

"Allow me to clarify, Ms. Stafford, Ms. Ross. We had to examine details of all your lives, including Tomas, even though I have known him for several years. Leonardo found that…"

I decide to tune out the rest of Dahvid's fancy blah, blah, blah. Instead, I zoom in on his features. It may appear as if I'm listening, but I'm definitely not! I'm so clever. Besides, I have no desire to be reminded of things I've worked so hard to forget.

Dahvid has a very different look from the other three guys. He has thick, black, wavy hair and olive skin, thick but defined eyebrows and curly eyelashes that go on forever. He has a pair of dimples that flank a million-dollar smile. My screen is gliding smoothly from red to orange into golden-yellow, passing through emerald green, landing on blue. Weird… I thought that color was only reserved for… Does this mean I like Dahvid's looks over Josef's?

Bleep!

Is it possible I could like them both, even if they're so different?

Chimes…

Would this discovery be considered art appreciation or betrayal?

Bleep!

Focus.

"Ms. Stafford?" I hear Dahvid say, interrupting my expert analysis of his movie star features. "Do you have any further questions on how we conducted our investigation on you and your team?"

"What was the last part, again?" I try faking my way out.

"Any questions?" He sounds a bit impatient— I know the feeling.

"Ms. Stafford, I can see that you are frustrated with the vetting process, but it is all about the final outcome. We are here to make your wishes for the world take place through our joint venture," Dahvid clarifies.

"I'm frustrated because the process seems rather one-sided. I don't like being put under a microscope. You have looked into our lives, but we know nothing about you or your invisible team!"

Bleep!

Rude.

"We respect everyone's need for privacy so we only looked into what would be pertinent to this mission, nothing more, nothing less. My apologies if you think we overstepped. This is a very dangerous time, we cannot afford to make a single mistake."

"Exactly my point!" I respond sarcastically.

Bleep!

Very Rude.

He takes a sip and adds, "Trust me, Tomas is extremely thorough, so if anyone was examined under a microscope, it was me," Dahvid remarks looking extra serious.

"What are you talking about?" I ask.

"Mr. Kesher is extremely protective of his friends, especially you. He discovered that our mothers roomed together at La Sorbonne, years before we were born."

Wait— What? Tomas researched Dahvid to protect— me, in spite of how rude and dismissive I am of him?

Chimes…

Great— just great! Now I'm not only furious but embarrassed. Could there be a worse combination? Wish I could stop this meeting altogether.

Bleep!

Apologize.

"I apologize for my slight overreaction," I share reluctantly.

"Slight overreaction?" Tomas repeats sarcastically.

Dahvid takes a deep breath, tugs at his sky collar and continues, "In conclusion, Leonardo and Jordan are confident that you, Ms. Stafford, possess the integrity and the conviction to lead us as a group, and change the world for the better."

"Are you ready to accept the position?" Tomas asks eagerly.

I regroup and say, "I can't accept anything right now, other than the compliment— thank you. First, I want to see Tomas's research. Fair is fair, facts are facts."

Chimes…

"I understand. No one should enter an agreement without reading the fine print first. You just demonstrated being an astute businesswoman. I am confident that Tomas will be glad to share his findings on yours truly. Here is a copy of our contract."

"Jazz, please read it thoroughly, make any changes you think are necessary," I instruct.

Jazz gives me a thumbs up.

What am I doing? It sounds like I'm accepting. I flash back to when I was captain of the debate team. I'd be terrible, no— horrible to my mates, when they wouldn't perform as I had expected. Even though I hated myself for it, I'd do it anyway.

How can I possibly accept to partner with this gentle, well-mannered guy and his invisible team? That bossy, demanding, perfectionist, dictator side of me is bound to resurface any minute. Accepting means risking that my microcosm could crumble. I'd be antagonizing my closest friends and losing my lifelong dream, forever! I don't want to be a miserable person, nor make everyone else miserable around me, either. What am I going to do? Wait— what's wrong? I'm shaking and hearing shrieking violins. It feels like the bottom is falling out from under me…

The screen is flashing deep red…

Bleep! Bleep! Bleep!

EMERGENCY ALERT
LOW BLOOD SUGAR
EAT — FOOD — NOW

The hypoglycemia alert is going off. Josef has experienced firsthand what happens when I ignore the symptoms. It's not pretty, not pretty at all. He reacts immediately and springs forward, as if I'm going through the Glåsse. "Jess, are you alright?" As he asks, I realize that the last thing I ate today was the energy drink served by that Southern Belle, whose flirtatious eyelashes could set off a *tsunami.* Those nutrients left my system hours ago. I can't afford to skip another meal, but I can't break away from the meeting either. What am I going to do?

The screen flashes red again…

EAT — FOOD — NOW

I walk over to the dresser and open the top drawer, where I keep my stash of emergency food. I go back to bed and start snacking on some home-made nut balls. "I can't do this…" I mumble with a mouth full.

"Pardon? I am having trouble understanding what you just said," Dahvid remarks.

"I said— I can't do this! I just can't!" I yell out, sounding desperate. My eyes are begging for Josef to take over. He gets the message.

"We need to take a break— immediately. Jessica needs to level her blood sugar."

"I understand, please, continue eating and we can resume the meeting."

"No, you really don't understand, we can't continue— not right now," Josef explains.

"Then allow me to make a suggestion," Dahvid requests.

"What're you trying to sell us nooow?" I whine.

"Jess...!" Jazz exclaims, getting ahead of the Bleep!

Dahvid blinks quickly and shares, "This presents an excellent opportunity to demo TAPS, the meeting is already within Tower."

Tomas interrupts. "They don't know about TAPS."

"Sorry, of course, thank you, Tomas." Dahvid flusters, "TAP stands for Time Acceleration Program, the S is for simulation. While we take a break, we can practically freeze the time we are in. The only condition is..."

"Another condition?" I blurt out with apple in my mouth.

Bleep!

Listen.

Dahvid inhales deeply, finishing his thought, "The only condition… is that we resume and complete this meeting tonight. That is all I needed to say."

I'm such a jerk when this blood sugar thing happens. Jazz knows the drill all too well. Josef has learned how to decipher my eye rolling and grunting. He wants this all to be over— quick.

Dahvid's gentle tone shifts to one of authority. "Activate your Micro Klôner and adjust the default to Tower so our team can get started."

My MK is on the top of the dresser, where I stash all my food. It's common for kids to have MK's in our rooms. We use them to produce all sorts of small items. The larger units, known as Klôners, produce more complex items, such as spare parts for home repairs and even certain appliances. The concept was originally inspired by a very successful recycling program about twenty years ago.

Discarded materials are reformulated and compressed into different sized cartridges, which get stored in temperature-controlled containers. The larger version, known as Mega Klôners, are able to create complete buildings in just a matter of hours.

Dahvid explains, "Before we begin, you will need to prepare a space where you can lie down. It can be a bed, sofa or even the floor. Use pillows to prop your head up by exactly thirty-six degrees. You will also need a leveled surface beside you. Your Micro Klôner is in the process of materializing a two-inch tall vial, containing two drops. Do not touch it or open it until instructed."

Jazz can't help but comment, "Isn't this the most adorably tiny little thing?"

"Now… pick the vial up carefully, and place it on the leveled surface next to you. Do not open it— the substance cannot be exposed to air. Without opening the top, squeeze the eye dropper so that it fills completely. Then, open it to dispense.

"Please be extremely careful to not underserve or waste the contents, because there are only two drops available per person for this trial run. Apply one drop to the right eye first, and then to the left— do not move your head during or right after. Put the top back on the vial when you finish. Once the process is over, store the empty closed dropper in a safe place. Any questions?"

"It's more of a comment— I don't like dispensing drops, I'm not good at it," Tomas complains.

"Just think— finally, we get to go into TAPS together. Give it a try," Dahvid shares warmly.

"You're right… I can do this… I hope," Tomas responds, then fakes a cough which prompts Dahvid into saying, "You may dispense the drops— now!"

After a brief pause he continues, "In a moment, your surroundings may appear different or distorted. Please, no sudden moves, you could damage something or injure yourself."

I hate not being able to see what everyone else is doing.

"Whoa… cool, so very cool…" Tomas shares, sounding much too animated over something.

"Tomas… please… shhh…" Jazz whispers.

I hear Dahvid speaking to someone, "I need to have a few words with you, so your TAPS experience has been programmed differently."

"Is there a problem?" Josef's deep voice responds with concern.

"Hopefully not. You know Ms. Stafford very well. She seems to be under a lot of stress…"

"What you're seeing is her intense personality being affected by extremely poor eating habits. But, that aside, she's the right person for this project."

"I have no doubt and I can tell how much you care about her. When you wake up, check on her and make sure she is up to the task. We need her to be focused and coherent. If she doesn't commit to leading us tonight, Leonardo will pull out of the deal. We have no time to waste. When you are ready, contact me so I can wake the others."

"We won't let you down," Josef responds.

Dahvid can tell that Josef cares… My heart is melting… Ewww… so is my room… it's liquifying… the Glåsse must be super-hot… my spheres… are oozing down the wall. Hope they don't stick to the floor cuz I'll never get them off…

POWERS

ACT VI

The sound of Josef's voice wakes me up, "Stef… Stefan?… Stéfano?" Seems he's having a hard time waking his brother. Wonder why I'm able to listen in.

"How was it? What're you feeling?" he asks.

Stefan replies, "Who knooows? What was I supposed to feel, anyway? How long did we sleep?"

"No idea. Not sure if I fell asleep, or if I just rested. It may not work on everybody."

"Maybe not. So what do you think about Dahvid and all this tech?" Stefan wonders.

"Impressive even though I'm not sure how it all works yet," Josef responds.

"D'you feel like you're spinning and have a band around your head?" Stefan asks.

"Oh maaan… exactly… Let's take it easy and stay in bed for a bit longer. I have to check on

Jess soon and make sure she's up for the meeting to continue."

"Good luck, she's in rare form today, she's…"

"Are you awake?" Josef is speaking to me. Good thing his brother didn't say more, it would be very hard to hide my embarrassment or my upset.

"Josef… hi, yeah, getting there." I yawn and stretch.

"Feeling better— I hope?" he asks.

"My head hurts— but not as much as it did when I rammed into your chin the day we met. Remember?"

"How could I forget? You made a lasting impression…" he replies, rubbing his jaw.

"Very funny… Is the meeting over yet?" I ask.

"Not quite… we took a break."

"So much for that dream coming true," I say sarcastically. "What about you? Did you guys get some sleep?"

Chimes…

Thoughtful.

"Unsure," Josef replies curtly.

I take a deep breath and say, "How is this thing with Dahvid going to work if you keep having to rescue me? What kind of a leader falls apart at every turn?"

"What do you mean? You're not falling apart at every turn. You're intense and have terrible eating habits, that's what complicates matters. Combine that with the fact that you're facing an existential crisis. There you have it— the perfect storm," he chuckles.

"Taking advanced psychology in 10th grade?"

He nods, "I just learned about this. Think about it— your greatest wishes and your greatest fears have collided."

"Hmm… that might explain why I'm confused and frustrated at the same time. I talk about making changes in the world, and when I have the chance to do it, I cave. What a fraud, I'm a disaster, an emotional weakling."

"Jessica Stafford— stop that! Those aren't your words. You're repeating what the media said about you last year!"

"They really got to me. Where's the warrior in me when we need her— where?" I feel like crying.

"Sorry, but I'm not joining your pity party. Let me know when it's over, and I'll come back," Josef snaps.

"No! Pleeease… don't go…" I beg.

He tries to cheer me up. "If you could reach for

a mirror— safely, you'd see that the warrior is right in front of you. You're really good at fighting other people's battles, but you're really bad at dealing with your own stuff. It boils down to one simple fact— you're scared."

"Are you ever afraid of your emotions?"

"I've learned to work through most things," he replies curtly.

"So how do I get there from here?"

"Start by admitting you're scared. Feel it; own it. Say it out loud. I'll be here to support you every step of the way. But believe me— the last thing you need is rescuing."

Since I can't move quickly, I have no choice but to wipe my teary face with the bed sheet.

"I could be persuaded to coach you— here and there," he quips, holding up a tissue box. I'm too embarrassed to smile.

"Jess, your golden opportunity has arrived. You've been selected, not to prove a point or win a trophy in a debate, but to devise plans that can change the world!"

"Well... I..."

"Shhh... just take it in," my newly self-appointed, personal coach instructs, placing his finger on his lips.

I grab onto the covers and pull them towards

my face, hiding everything but my eyes. It feels as if I'm grabbing on to the handrail of a roller coaster for dear life.

"Josef, I… it's really hard to feel feelings I don't like feeling."

I sense eucalyptus and lavender, what perfectly perfect timing. I exhale, close my eyes and imagine tiny little leaf buds pushing through the crusty, dark tree bark in early Spring. "If they can do it, so can I!" I exclaim. Josef is staring at me with those expressive blue eyes of his.

"Okay, here goes: I'm scared because the mission sounds really exciting, but I'm really overwhelmed at the same time. It's way too much responsibility."

"Deep inside, you know you want this."

"Do I?… I guess I do but so much is at risk."

"There's much more at risk— if you decline," he clarifies.

If he only knew what I meant. The thought of pushing him and everyone else away in the process of changing the world is what terrifies me the most. Well, almost as much as dealing with The World Ogre. I nod a few times during my inner conversation.

Josef misinterprets my actions and considers them as an acceptance.

"Excellent! Looks like we can let Dahvid know we're ready to resume the meeting."

"Nooo… I'm not…" I try to stop him.

Dahvid welcomes us back and is eager to know if we feel refreshed and rested. I can't help but notice that Tomas's face looks unusually relaxed. Jazz is glowing, as she arranges her swirly, whirly cinnamon locks, securing a loose bun on the top of her head. She's used a set of red, black and gold enamel chop sticks Stefan gave her. Good strategy. He's handsomely transfixed.

Dahvid tries hard not to be distracted by her movements and announces, "We are ready to continue. Ms. Stafford, there are a couple of stipulations we need to cover next."

"Stipulations?" I ask.

"To be at the helm of this project, it will be necessary to keep things… shall we say… undercover from family and friends."

Between bites, I respond, "Keeping things from my parents hasn't paid off lately, but in this case, what's my choice? What good friends are you referring to other than Maarlee? We can't involve her, she's way too busy helping the world in her own way."

Dahvid starts humming a familiar tune. He's handsome— and he sings too? I'm in trouble—

real trouble.

Bleep!

Focus.

"Ohhh… you mean Sahrit? Why would I involve her in something like this?"

"Her popularity would be quite an asset. The problem is that due to the delicate nature of this mission, you would not be able to divulge all the details. Are you comfortable with that?"

"No way! I couldn't leave her out of it. Sahrit supported me the moment we met. Besides, we already have a business partnership," I explain. "And another thing— she'd pick up on my anxiety, immediately. She sees right through me."

"So how could we resolve this dilemma?"

Dahvid looks handsome when he's thinking.

Bleep!

Focus.

"If I were to accept, having her involved would be absolutely sensational. Who else could be a better spokesperson for our generation?"

"Alright!" Tomas exclaims, "Dahvid— looks like we're done here!"

"Wait a minute— not so fast, I haven't accepted yet!" I snap.

Dahvid adds, "I happen to agree. Sahrit would be a tremendous asset to our initiative. If I asked she might accept, we happen to know each other quite well. In fact, we are not only friends but…"

I feel a deep throb of jealousy in my back.

Bleep!

"…we're business collaborators," Dahvid admits joyfully.

"I hate being lied to and tricked!" I blurt out, raising my voice.

Bleep!

Unfounded.

"Jessica Stafford watch your words!" Jazz is pretty upset that I've lost my cool— again. On top of that, I can tell by Tomas's expression, that he's extremely disappointed. All his hard work is crumbling. Well, that's just too bad! I can't protect him! I can barely handle my own emotions right now, let alone his.

Bleep!

Ungrateful. Selfish.

"It's well-known fact that I hate being told what to do and being pressured into something."

Bleep!

Insufficient. Apologize.

"Sorry for being so selfish and inconsiderate."

Chimes…

Tomas smirks. "I always feel pressured."

"Oh Tomas…" Jazz sighs, with a heavy heart.

"Ms. Stafford, please accept my apologies if you felt lied to or tricked. That was not my intention. You just expressed what you stand for, who is important to you and why. That only solidifies why we want you to lead us."

This guy sure knows how to work around my temperamental outbursts and my ego. Wonder if he has sisters.

Bleep!

Focus.

Right on cue, Flower Power starts playing softly in the background. "Wow! Sahrit!"

"Surprise!" she exclaims, blushing shyly.

My bad mood evaporates once I see her. She's so natural and sincere, even in her appearance. She wears no makeup or very little, but only when she's on stage. Her glossy dark brown hair goes down to her waist. Usually, she'll wear fun hats or flowers, a headband with shells or ribbons or something funky like a hippie from the 1970's. But not today, she's just her beautiful Latina, Persian self.

"Sahrit! Did you know we were going to be at the same meeting?"

She looks a bit embarrassed. "Yes and no. Dahvid invited me to join in, but I didn't know when I'd have access to enter. So please continue, I don't want to stop the river of creativity from flowing. Keep going as if I'd been here the whole time."

Sahrit is so humble…

Chimes…

"If you'd been here the whole time, you'd know it's been like a choppy storm at high sea more than a flowing river," Tomas divulges.

Tomas can be so clever…

Chimes…

Dahvid beams, "We are getting ready to discuss some ideas for a joint project. We think you would be a perfect fit."

Jazz breaks in, "Before you get into all that, I suggest, that as a group, we come up with a way to encapsulate what we each bring to the table and/or want to accomplish. That will help develop our mission statement."

"Excellent idea! Who would like to start?" Dahvid asks, enthusiastically.

"I'll be formatting everyone's ideas, save me till the end," Jazz adds.

I take a deep breath and say, "Before any of this, I need to say something…"

Dahvid welcomes me to the virtual podium.

"Should I accept to lead this group— I'd need reassurance that no physical or emotional harm will come to any of us nor to our families. I believe that loyalty is rewarded with loyalty." I pause to take a deep breath. I'm feeling feelings I'd rather not feel right now. "I've never, nor will I ever hurt or violate anyone's trust— intentionally, especially those who have supported me in hard times. Ufff… that was really tough, but I feel safe with you."

Josef is smiling his smile; Jazz and Sahrit are wiping tears from their sparkling eyes. Stefan is glowing, but because he's still transfixed on Jazz. Tomas and Dahvid look quite pleased.

Where would I be without my friends? Who would I be without them? How could I even consider walking away from everyone, especially my loyal followers on Liberty World?

"Accepting is a huge responsibility!" I blurt out.

Josef jumps in, "Hear, hear! We'll consider that your acceptance speech. It's unanimous! Jessica is the right person for the job!"

Everyone responds by cheering, whistling and applauding. "Thank you, everyone, but… I still haven't accepted— officially."

"This— is— absolutely— ridiculous, Jessica!" Tomas proclaims, hitting his desk with his fists. He's reached his limit. Who can really blame the guy?

Dahvid is more intrigued than annoyed. "You seem to be right on the verge. What is holding you back from accepting?"

Josef coaxes me, "Go ahead, Jess… just say it out loud."

"Alright… here goes… time to try on my softer side."

"You have a softer side?" Tomas emphasizes my words.

"She's trying to show her vulnerability," Jazz translates, "I know you can relate…" He nods and looks down.

I clear my throat, "Since your group has investigated my life, you're aware that I was dragged into the limelight and paid dearly for it. I don't want to experience that ever again, or put my parents or friends through that nightmare. You may have also noticed that… I don't handle pressure, criticism or stress very well, either. I'm still working through issues."

"If I misunderstood your passion, conviction and desire to repair the world through your debates, I apologize," Dahvid says, seemingly disappointed.

"I do feel passion, conviction and a desire to repair the world. But based on what I've gone through, what makes everyone here think I'd want to go through that again? Why would I want to risk…" my voice cracks.

"To risk what?" Josef helps.

"…losing all of you." I cover my mouth, but it's too late.

"Keep going," Josef whispers.

"The truth is… I care more about all of you than getting rid of The Ogre."

"Caring is what's behind many impressive masterminds and leaders," Dahvid replies reassuringly.

"One for all and all for one," comes from Stefan.

It's overwhelming, there's so much going on inside me. Should I laugh or should I cry? Uhh… ohh… seems the decision has been made, my sobbing is uncontrollable. My whole body is hurting from the effort. Should I cover my face or hug myself. Of all times, what must everyone be thinking of me now? Look at her, she's a fraud, a weakling, all talk— very little action. What a total disappointment. On the other hand, maybe showing emotional weakness could be a good strategy. If Dahvid thinks I'm imbalanced, his group might find someone else to play the part of the The

Chosen One, other than me.

Bleep!

Step up. They want you.

If only Dahvid would announce he's got to go, I'd be so relieved. My life would go back to normal. Whatever that means? The group is looking at me, completely baffled because I go from crying to laughing in a nanosecond. Is this a nervous breakdown? Tomas is becoming more and more disturbed by my behavior. He's holding his head, covering his ears, looking down, and rocking in his seat. Tomas has been actively searching for ways to repair the world and protecting me at the same time. He's been diligent, humble and private, while I'm just a big talker who doesn't really do much. That's it! I need to do something!

Chimes…

With regained composure and clarity, I clear my throat and say, "Mr. Kesher, can you hear me?"

He nods, still looking down.

"Please look at your device," I instruct.

He reluctantly removes his hands away from his ears and goes from frowning to smiling.

Chimes…

"What does it say, Tomas?" Jazz asks,

innocently. He can only whisper the answer.

"*Pardon, mon ami*? We could not hear you," Dahvid remarks.

"She accepts— she says she accepts!" he yells out.

I mouth, "Thank you, Tomas."

He's shedding a tear because of what I wrote?

Chimes…

Whoa… I can't believe how much this means to him. Wishing not to impose any more attention or uncomfortable emotions upon either of us, I request that we move on. Tomas seems to radiate— joy? I never knew he had that in him. Up until now I'd only experienced him as a brilliant, yet annoying and rather challenging personage in my life. Glad I found a way to thank him for putting up with me for so long and having so much faith in me. What a relief that the decision part is over.

Chimes…

Dahvid is eager to speak. "Ms. Stafford, our team is extremely pleased, to say the least. We have received clearance to proceed, therefore we need to present another of Leonardo's phenomenal contributions. It combines ocular and auditory nano implants, which are able to stream what others are seeing and hearing."

"I'd be interested in learning more about the recognizance and surveillance aspects of that tech. Are you saying that we'll be able to get into someone's head?" Josef remarks.

"Into— The— Chancellor's— head?" Stefan follows.

"Yes," Dahvid responds, matter-of-factly.

"That's got to be the darkest, loneliest place, ever. No way I'd want to go in there, not even with bodyguards," Sahrit quips.

"What's the process to make that happen?" I ask, brushing off my girlfriend's comment.

"There is highly specialized training involved, although the implementation of the tech itself is the easiest part of the whole process. It involves applying a series of drops in the subject's eyes, ears..."

"That sounds quite familiar," Tomas remarks.

"Who could get away with doing that to *Le Grande Ogre*?" Jazz asks with a French accent.

"Ahh... that is one of the many beautiful opportunities afforded by being in TAP, *Mademoiselle*. In this type of scenario, the person receiving the treatment would not be aware of it— at all. There may be a temporary bother, like itching or slight burning, minor discomforts. Nothing more than that."

"Fascinating" Josef affirms.

"Well… in that case… who wants to pay The Chancellor a visit?" Jazz exclaims, jokingly.

She gets no answer because the guys are already involved in an animated conversation on how to manage streams of consciousness. They want to be able to gain access to key players involved in specialized interactions throughout the world.

When they get to the part of including various members of government in our country, I jump in, "Guys?" They ignore me. "Guuuyyss!" I yell out. "Stop for a second!"

They glare at me, annoyed by the interruption. "All this conjecture is great, but we don't even have a mission statement yet. Let's put the plan of action on pause until then."

Dahvid shines his million-dollar smile. "She's right, we need help staying focused."

"Me— keeping others focused? Now that's hilarious," I chuckle, "if anyone can keep us focused here, it's Jazz. Therefore, I'd like to nominate her as our project manager. She'd be terrific at it. Besides, she'd be the first girl in Mr. Toledano's team."

"And here I thought I already had the job," Jazz jokes with a playful huff. "Why else would I be doing all this work— and for free?" She laughs her wonderful laugh.

"See what I mean, Dahvid? She's on top of everything, whether we want her to be or not!"

"In that case, Ms. Ross, would you also consider helping establish a network that would monitor all the interactions resulting from the surveillance implantation?" Dahvid requests.

"*Certainement monsieur!*" Jazz responds.

"Would this be a streaming agency that could transmit what's occurring in real time?" I ask.

"Yes, precisely, with TAP we can adjust to any time, no problem," Dahvid responds.

Jazz is ecstatic, "That's beyond ultra, mega, super cool! A media studio where people can function as directors and editors. It's like having a theatre and cinema production company, all rolled up in one!"

"We are pleased you accepted; we thought the position would fit you like a glove. It seems to check the boxes of many of your interests, including efficiency, tech and space planning," Dahvid explains.

"I'm getting this fabulous job... without even auditioning? Really?" Jazz remarks.

Tomas jumps in, "Are you kidding? You've been auditioning for this your whole life!"

"Wowow... thank you for making me a part of

such a wonderful opportunity. Tomas, you're a gem of a friend. Dahvid, thank you as well for the recognition. Since we'll be working so closely, I'd like if you called me Jazz… like the music."

"My friends call me Jess," I interrupt.

Bleep!

Spotlight stealing.

"Thank you, ladies. I am not accustomed to calling someone by their first name, unless it is offered— 'old school' upbringing. You know? If I go back to using last names, you will know why…"

What does that mean? Josef and Stefan don't seem quite as pleased with our friendly exchange as Jazz and I are. Stefan's getting antsy. His jealousy meter is rising fast.

"Getting back to business… the mission statement?" Jazz recommends.

"As you will soon find out, Jazz is phenomenal at encapsulating complex thoughts, making them brief and relatable."

Chimes…

Jazz bows her head regally, her graceful move inspires me. I'm going to handle leadership differently. Let's start the process by handing out compliments instead of commands. "I'd like to share how I envision each of you, and how that would fit into our mission," I announce. Okay… so far so good, everyone is smiling with anticipation.

Chimes…

Uh, oh… spoke too soon… everyone, except for Tomas.

I request a moment off-camera to prepare my next move. I slide off the bed slowly and go to the hallway closet, walking on bare tippy toes. Perfect— the old suitcase filled with childhood treasures is still on the top shelf. I reach for it, place it on the floor and open it. Ah! my prized possession. After giving it a quick kiss, I place it behind my back, return and sit back in bed.

"Thank you for that, I'm ready. Tomas, I'd like to start with you."

Poor guy, he looks downright petrified, as if he's bracing for something terrible to happen. I've traumatized him with my putdowns and criticisms. Hope this makes a difference.

"Tomas, you've more than proven an outstanding ability to absorb information, identifying what's needed to solve a problem, and locating the talent capable of creating a solution."

He goes from slouching to sitting up straight. His frown becomes a smirk and he tilts his head like a curious puppy.

Chimes…

"You are a loyal friend and a committed listener. So for your absolutely brilliant work, dedication and loyalty…," I bring my childhood magic wand forward. I plan to use it in lieu of a medieval sword to knight him.

"Tomas Kesher, I dub thee Master Head Connector." The wand appears to tap each of his shoulders.

Everyone cheers, whistles and applauds.

Tomas is blushing and smiling as he gives us a royal wave. He can be funny— sometimes.

Chimes…

Wow, recognizing others for their efforts makes me feel really good.

Bleep!

Not about you.

We're going to be a wonderrific team; we're going to change the world. Think I'll use the knighting wand on everyone.

Chimes…

"For brokering the tech talent and managing challenging situations, for being respectful, patient, ethical and professional, Dahvid Toledano, I dub thee, Director of Tech and

Business Protocol."

"Such an honor, thank you," he bows, humbly, placing his right hand on his heart as he receives the virtual knighting.

Josef needs to be next. I'd hate to hurt his feelings.

Chimes…

"Responsibility, loyalty, discipline, and great focus are required for the implementation of intelligence. There's no one better qualified at identifying those needs than you, Josef Tallon-Saldane, I dub thee, Director of Security and Intelligence Operations."

His salute only emphasizes that supremely handsome, chiseled face. My screen quickly shifts to blue.

"All effective commanders are supported by experts in their field. Someone who excels at anticipating and planning squad formations and maneuver efficacy. Stefan Tallon-Saldane, I dub thee, Chief of Staff and Strategic Fulfillment."

He salutes, presenting a handsome, brunette, green-eyed version of his older brother.

"To gain and maintain support for future endeavors, we need a trusted and admired spokesperson, someone who represents all that is true and good. For your ability to speak eloquently through the universal language of music, Sahrit Bana, I dub thee, Director of Public Relations and Communication."

Tearing freely, she creates a heart with her hands and fingers.

"Order and logic are required for a well-oiled machine to function properly. Patience, understanding and intuition are essential. What challenges or baffles many is natural for Jazz Ross. I dub thee, Chief System Manager, Director of Heart and Soul." Jazz hugs herself as if she's hugging me.

"We're developing a dangerous mission that will bring us tons of stress and anxiety. Therefore, I propose that Jazz and Sahrit, establish The Zen Force," I add.

"What is that, exactly?" Stefan wonders.

"They will provide calming techniques to fit each of our group members' needs," I reply confidently. "It's likely that I'll be calling on them— often."

Sahrit, our hippie chick smiles and creates V-shaped peace signs with both hands.

Dahvid looks so pleased by this. "Jess, your vision is so thorough, seems you have covered… almost everything."

"Thank you, Dahvid. Wait— did you say almost?" A heavy dark cloud of self-doubt descends upon me. What did I miss? I panic.

Bleep!

Breathe.

Dahvid responds, "We have talked about so many things, it probably slipped your mind. I trust that you have taken this highly important element into account?"

"I'm checking my notes… and… no— I don't see any elements missing," I reply.

Bleep!

Humility.

Dahvid clears his throat and reaches for his thermos. After a couple of big gulps he says, "Our plans will be on a grand scale, requiring substantial funding. Where do you see those funds coming from? Who have you chosen as your Financial Minister?" Dahvid inquires.

I'm beyond humiliated by the extent of my ineptitude. So much for big picture thinking. How could I have been so stupid? How could I have forgotten a tiny detail like— finances? This proves my point, I'm a big talker that never meant to change the world. Case closed!

Bleep!

Stop negative talk.

Josef pushes for an answer, "What are your thoughts on funding, Jess?"

He likes me because I can get myself out of any jamb, well… this may be the exception.

"It so happens that… when one specializes in big picture visualizations… the expense of the operation such as this… is never quantified down to the dollar. It's more of a progressive and expansive process… Does that make sense?"

Stefan groans and rolls his eyes while Josef replies, "Understandable. What did you allow for it initially, then? We can always adjust it as we solidify the details."

"Dahvid, may I have a sip of whatever's in your thermos? I only ask because it seems to give you courage, and that's what I need right now," I remark nervously.

Dahvid smiles and places his thermos close to the screen, just as eucalyptus comes to the rescue. I take a deep breath and say, "Okay, I admit it, I never considered the expense of such an enormous operation… because I never thought any of this could really happen."

Chimes…

"But that's all you ever talk about, and besides, you're involved in global business! How could you not think of funding?" Stefan doubles down.

The debate megastar in me comes out of

retirement by breaking the most basic rule of engagement. I attack my opponent. "Back off, Bud!"

Bleep!

Unacceptable.

Grrr… I'm so angry— mostly at myself. I close my eyes for a moment, trying to calm down. "Let's consider the facts, shall we? I'm a fourteen-year-old girl with a bountiful imagination, who talks a lot about her big ideas. Out of nowhere, a group of people I've never heard of expect me to devise an elaborate and detailed plan, in a matter of hours, to dethrone the most powerful and feared man on Planet Earth. Am I correct so far, sir?"

Stefan's eyes get huge.

"Well— am I?" I repeat.

He can only nod.

"So you— a guy who talks about war in the comfort and safety of a climate controlled classroom, expects— me to have this all figured out— just like that?" I say, snapping my fingers at him.

"Jess, you don't want to go there. It's getting out of hand," Josef remarks.

Sahrit, the peacemaker, jumps in, "Even if we are superhumans, and we have businesses, it doesn't mean we know everything and that we're good at it all. We're contributing with our talents so why not with part of our earnings?" she shares innocently.

"Seriously?" Stefan smirks, turning to his brother, inviting him to mock Sahrit's idea.

Jazz is supremely annoyed, "Stefan, what's so funny about chipping in? Her idea has great potential."

Stefan speaks up, "I don't find her idea funny— I find it ridiculous! None of you have the slightest concept of what's entailed in running a military operation."

Tomas cuts in, wanting to be part of the pushy boy's club, "Yeah, she'd have to sell a million, billion, trillion, quadrillion, quintillion more songs to make a dent in the expenses for this kind of a mission. Right?"

Why does he have to use that tone? It drives me up the wall and out the window!

Jazz takes over. "We're here to learn from each other. So bring it down— all of you!"

Knowing better than to interfere, Dahvid sips quietly as he watches our dynamics unfold.

My bubblegram to Jazz says, "Look at what my incompetence has provoked. I should have shameless incompetence in my hue.r.u..."

Dahvid requests that we discuss this in a civil manner. Tomas responds by saying that Stefan doesn't know how to be civil because he's in the military. No one laughs, even though his pun is clever, it couldn't have come at a worse time.

Josef thinks he can help by saying, "Confidence is a virtue, overconfidence tends to get people in trouble."

Stefan cuts in, "Thought the only philosophy teacher we had was at the academy."

"I sense some hostility, gentlemen. Would you care to solve this off Tower before we move on?" Dahvid suggests.

"Sorry for the disruption, Dahvid. This matter will be resolved later— privately." Josef is sounding very frustrated because Stefan and Tomas ignore him and are still at it. Jazz excuses herself for a moment.

"Owowouch! What's going on? Where's the fire?" I yell out, pressing down on my ears from the pain. After a few short trills, the torture stops. Jazz returns with her dad's old lacrosse coaching whistle still between her teeth. She releases it, letting it dangle from a cord around her neck. "That's some fashion statement, *Mademoiselle Rossé*," I remark.

Dahvid thanks her for the charming, low tech solution towards conflict resolution.

Uh… ohh… another guy has fallen under Jazz's spell. Stefan isn't happy, not happy at all. Hope he doesn't start showing his jealousy and competitiveness. It really hurts his one and only family member.

Sahrit resorts to the universal language of music to get rid of any leftover static, inspiring Josef and Dahvid to team up. They regain control of the meeting. Dahvid believes that being a dynamic dreamer is my greatest gift. Josef follows by declaring that this group's purpose is to support one another and solidify our vision.

My mind is blown by how these two great guys work so well together. Do I have good taste or what? My screen takes on a heightened, never-before-seen shade of blue.

Dahvid sips a couple of times from his bottomless thermos and tells us that unless we are fully invested in this project, it won't fly. We have to feel deep down inside that repairing the world means everything to us. We have to find ways to prove our willingness by giving of ourselves, not just of our earnings. He assures us that if we manage to accomplish this, the financial assistance will find its way to us.

Stefan is back to his polite self. "What is our timeframe from plan and fulfillment?"

I jump in, "I'd like to shed some light on this one.

We should have seven to ten days left of 'implant battery life' after they're disabled. This way we'll have more time to do what's needed. Then we'll go back to default— the thought of that petrifies me."

Bleep!

Betrayal.

Whaat? Why? Oh nooo! I just shared Dad's secret. I'm petrified— and so ashamed.

"What does being back in default really mean, anyway?" Tomas is getting nervous.

"How could you possibly know anything about a reserve? Is this another one of your visionary theories?" Stefan remarks.

"No! It's not a theory. The info comes from a 100% reliable source!"

"Who is it?" Josef pushes for an answer. "I've done extensive research on this matter, there's nothing to support what you're saying."

"It's in a journalist's code of ethics not to share one's sources— I learned that from Maarlee," I snap back.

"Sorry, but since you're not a journalist and you can't back your statement with solid data, we have to disregard it. We will be operating as expected— on empty. That's final!" Josef proclaims.

"Yes, sir!" I reply and salute.

Well, that's that. At fifteen, this junior cadet superhero is the oldest in our group and he also has the deepest voice. I foresee he'll be pulling rank— a lot, during the mission. Even though his response hurts, I have to remind myself this is not about me.

Chimes…

"We need to come up with a solid plan— now!" Stefan exclaims, trying to emulate his brother's commanding tone.

I'm amused by the thought of my greatest fear: scaring my friends away by being too much of an Alpha Female. Ha! Joke's on me.

Jazz indicates by clearing her throat that she wants to speak, "Ladies and gents, I'd like to share a concept that could be helpful as we adjust to new types of sensations. Your team could design this using the right materials."

Dahvid is intrigued by the specs of a thin band worn on ring fingers. They'd provide sensory signals that would otherwise be lost once the implants are disabled. "Jazz, you are absolutely brilliant! They can be made from graphene and produced via Micro Klôner."

Studying her professional looking sketches, my mind can't help but wander to Zivah Zahav's soulful jewelry line and her inventive use of graphene.

Chimes… Bleep!

Good. Focus.

That's new, a combo thought interrupter. I'm making progress.

"That's a spectacular idea!" I exclaim.

Sahrit is so excited, she'll be endorsing the rings. "Jazz… would you consider giving me your input on wardrobe for this weekend's concert? It's an important one… I have some ideas but… I'd love to invite you as my guest. You'd have backstage access before, during and after the show. That is… if you don't have any plans, already."

Jazz is in heaven and responds with, "Oh my stars… how exciting— yes— no plans— thank you!"

Uh, ohhh… Stefan looks like he's about to…

"What's the point of going if you're going to be backstage? It's the worst seat in the house!" he shouts.

Josef's hand slams down on his brother's shoulder, "Stop!"

Stefan's jealousy always gets the best of him. Poor guy, he wears his feelings about Jazz on his sleeve. Wonder if his heart gets badly bruised every time he falls for her flirtatious games. Sure hope someday, someone is crazy-gugu-gaga over me like he is over her.

Bleep!

Focus.

Jazz ignores Stefan completely. She's much more interested in Dahvid's comments. "Thanks to all your preliminary research, *Mademoiselle*, the team can go straight to producing code for the rings. In just a few minutes, you will all have one."

Tomas seems to be in another world. His arms are positioned as if he's holding a guitar, his fingers are moving gracefully over invisible strings.

Stefan jumps in, "Hey, man, you're not serious? There's no way I'm wearing a ring." Josef nods in agreement. "Yeah— no, that won't work for us."

"Gentlemen, we have to be flexible about wearing externals. The ring will be practically imperceptible, no wider than a few strands of hair," Dahvid explains.

"Thought you guys were so brave? What happened? Are you scared of wearing a tiny little ring?" Jazz taunts them with a sassy tone.

"It should work. I was worried it could have been a hinderance, especially during one of my daily activities, one of which is of great importance," Tomas shares, all in one breath.

Playing guitar is of great importance to him?

Bleep!

"Make sure to program the same codes you currently use in hue.r.u. Please— I cannot stress this enough— do not divulge this information to anyone!" Dahvid instructs.

"If I had a dollar for every time someone has said that, we'd have enough money to fund this whole thing," I giggle.

The Micro Klôners have done their job. Jazz is the first to comment, "Dahvid! Designing with you and your team is a dream come true, talk about immediate gratification!"

Stefan and Josef reluctantly admit the rings aren't so bad, after all. "Excellent business strategy, Ms. Ross!" I exclaim.

Dahvid smiles warmly, "We accomplished more than I expected tonight. If you will excuse me…" he fails to swallow a yawn. "In the last thirty-six hours, I haven't had much sleep, we can continue tomorrow."

"Was that in TAP or regular time?" Stefan remarks, "how long did we sleep for, anyway?"

Before Dahvid can answer, Tomas cuts in to explain, "We slept slightly over three hours in TAP. With a ratio of approximately, two hundred to one, including the second portion of the meeting, that was one to one and a half minutes in regular time— tops!"

"Interesting," Josef remarks. I can see his wheels spinning at warp speed.

"Thank you for that, Tomas, I could not have explained it better myself." Dahvid's voice is fading fast.

Jazz raises her hand and waves, "Uuu… Before you go, I've got a great idea!" Dahvid nods and motions for her to speak.

She spreads her hands, forming a banner in the air, 'Beauty Sleep Skin Care, Healthy Solutions For Exhausted Women.'

Even though Dahvid is pretty frazzled, he can't help but smile. Jazz is excited he likes the idea, "Since we can provide deep sleep in a short amount of time, why not market it?"

"That is very clever, unfortunately, Leonardo has made one thing crystal clear. We cannot use this technology for anything other than removing The World Chancellor from power."

"Are you sure? I already drew the label for it and everything," Jazz pouts, looking forlorn.

Dahvid takes what must be the very last drop of whatever is left in his thermos, "Hold on to the design. I have a feeling we'll be using it in the very near future." Jazz is happy again.

A statement shows up on the screen:

Monday March 4, 2041 7:00 AM
Expect to wake refreshed.
Meeting resumes 8:30 AM.
TAP proficiency requires
a balanced diet.

That's so perfectly perfect! TAP is what I've been waiting for. That's my motivation. It's bound to improve my health and my lovely disposition.

Chimes…

"Dahvid, I know you're exhausted, but may I say a couple of things before we sign off?" Dahvid nods at me in agreement.

"My sincere thanks to you and your team for entrusting us with this phenomenal tech. A special thank you for putting up with my crazy mood swings. The TAP diet will make a huge difference. I just know it."

Chimes…

He nods again and disappears.

In the process of adjusting to regular time, my Glåsse takes on an indescribable turquoise. The mesmerizing color provokes me to tears, but not tears of sadness, but of relief.

Jazz must know what's going on with me, her

73

sphere is drifting in. The pale pink over my gorgeous turquoise creates the most delicate lavender shadow. What a beautiful backdrop for her latest work of art: the Flower Power logo.

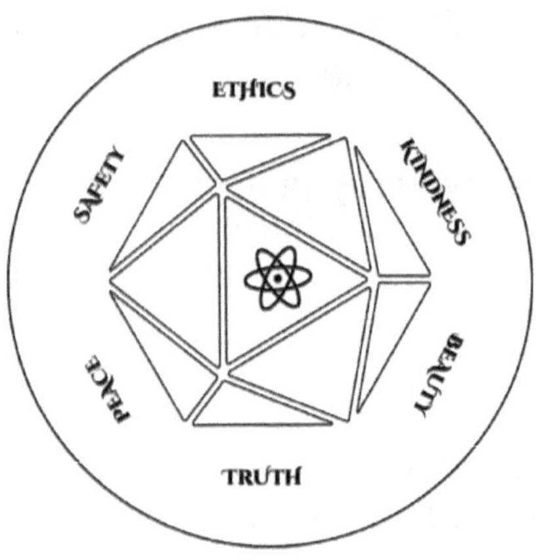

SHOWERS
ACT VII

Amazing, this is the first time, in I don't know how long, I haven't needed a multi-phased alarm to wake up. Incredible to feel rested and coherent this early.

"As of this morning, I vow to never ignore you again," I say rubbing my growling tummy. "I take care of you— you take care of me."

Chimes…

Since it's early, I may even get my fair share of breakfast today. I gallop downstairs. My mouth waters with anticipation.

"Good morning, Sweetheart," Mom says, joyfully, "you look so well rested and already dressed, too! What can I get you?"

"Anything that Jake hasn't eaten yet— I'm famished!"

"You're in luck. We're going to let him sleep in today," Mom announces.

"That's the best news I've heard all day," I reply cheerfully.

Dad laughs at my 7:15 AM joke.

My parents are shocked, watching me prepare what I plan to scarf down in one sitting. Since I'm new at the eating healthy thing, guessing quantity is important. I'll start by stacking six fluffy pancakes, butter between the layers and warm maple syrup poured on top, slowly. Can't eat them until the golden square on the top melts away. In the meantime, my side plate gets a mound of scrambled eggs with a large scoop of grated *Manchego* cheese. One of the glasses already has milk in it and the other, my customized, fresh squeezed orange juice. Mom strains out the pulp and saves it just for me. I love popping all those delicious little pouches.

The morning feast is consumed. "That was super delicious, Mom, thank you," I say, reclining in my seat and wiping my mouth with a soft fabric napkin. Even though my tummy isn't growling anymore, I'm still needing something else. My oculars zero in on the hand-painted bowl that Jazz made for us, it's overflowing with fresh fruit. Next to it are a couple of freshly baked banana bread loaves, still cooling off. Mom adds a tray of carefully crafted, individually wrapped energy bars, to her gastronomic exhibit. I need to be proactive and grab some of them now, or I'll regret it later. After last night's fiasco, my emergency food reservoir is completely empty. My parents are smiling with delight.

"Whaaat?" I ask, pretending to be annoyed.

"Nothing, nothing at all. Everything's just wonderful! We haven't seen you eat with such pleasure since, well… before… you know…" Dad blurts out. Mom grabs his wrist. He stops.

"We're thrilled to see you making up for the skipped meals yesterday. We saw all the alerts you ignored," Mom remarks.

"Oh, yeah, that— lesson learned— believe me. But also… since Jake is asleep, it's only fair that I get to eat like a jock," I reply while filling a metal mesh basket with snacks. Mom and Dad chuckle at the sight. It's so nice to hear them laugh at the mention of my brother's name. Lately, it's only been a source of arguments and lots of crying. I give them each a peck on the cheek and run back upstairs.

"Good morning, MK," I say to the Micro Klôner on top of my old dresser. I open the top drawer to replenish my provisions.

At exactly 8:30, Dahvid appears, welcoming us back. "Did everyone sleep well?"

I'm the first to volunteer my report, "Slept well, woke up alert, ate enough to feed an army."

He gives me thumbs up and a proud smile.

"My sleep experience was dreamy," Jazz responds playfully. "And yours, Dahvid?"

"Much needed… thank you for asking," his smile fades as he regrets having to inform us that the plans for today must change. The announcement is received with moans and groans of disappointment.

"We can still get together to practice TAP today, only it will change from morning to afternoon."

"But whyyy?" Jazz whines, sounding like a spoiled little girl who can't get what she wants.

He pauses and takes a deep breath, "We've just gotten word…   The World Chancellor is demanding that everyone, eight to eighteen must have our implants disabled— today!"

"Whaaat— so soon?" I say, shaking.

Tomas starts rocking back and forth, holding his head and repeating, "No— no— no!"

"What're we going to do?" Sahrit asks, crying. Jazz is silent.

"We must try our best to remain calm. The sooner we go through the deactivation process, the sooner we can get to work. After we hear the announcement, we will have a plan of action in place." Dahvid sounds shaky.

I make a weak attempt to calm Tomas by empathizing with his fears, "We'll be okay, Tomas, remember, we have a reserve, it will wear off gently and…"

Josef interrupts me, "Jess— stop!"

One thing is for Intelly to put me in my place, but Josef? Even though he's second in command, I don't like it, I don't like it at all.

Dahvid clears his throat so he can read us a statement just in, from Leonardo.

"Greetings Collaborators, today was slated to be a memorable day and so shall it remain. Though there will be challenges ahead, ultimately we will reflect on this day as a time of growth. Appreciate all of today's events, minute by minute and hour by hour. Prepare to experience emotional and physical drain, even some depression. Do not repress it, discount it or avoid it. Be sure and discuss things among yourselves first, then with your family. To remarkable transitions, Leonardo."

Dahvid reminds us to not discuss any topics regarding TAP with anyone other than each other. Our military branch appears to be more stoic than usual. Their training must include hiding emotion in the face of adversity— most of the time. In contrast, the rest of us are feeling frantic. Jazz and Sahrit decide it's a good time to expand on the benefits of being in touch with our feelings and emotions. In a classic Jessica move of 'don't tell me what to do'— I do the opposite of what Leonardo suggested. I tune out. I'm not good at this feelings stuff, so what's the point of learning how to tune into it now?

Bleep!

"Ladies, thank you for your valuable feedback. We will be in contact about when to reconvene later in the day." Dahvid gets interrupted by Sahrit.

"Oh noo…! Please… noo! Dahvid!" she cries.

"What's wrong?" he yells back.

"I was just contacted by an official from the WLC. They're instructing all companies worth eight million dollars and up, owned by anyone under age eighteen to… to give them… full access… to… our financial records." She's trying to speak between sobs.

"How dare they?" I scream. "They've been meddling in our lives, under the radar, all along. Now they're letting us know they'll be doing it openly? As of when…?"

"The law… enters into effect… at midnight…"

I'm so upset, my screen is throbbing volcanic bright red.

"Makes sense they'd roll out all kinds of things today. Didn't you hear? It's the First Annual Let's Completely Disempower Hybrids Day!" Tomas exclaims with unfamiliar fury.

"There's more," Sahrit expands. "No one under the age of eighteen can have full control over their own business either. It can't be in our own name nor transferred to a relative with the same last name as ours."

"It was bad enough when we were forced to hire someone over eighteen to manage our finances— and now this?" Jazz is outraged.

Sahrit is shaking like a leaf. "What am I going to do? If they take away all my earnings— how will I be able to help all the children in underdeveloped countries?"

Her heart is as big as the universe. Incredible what came to her first— helping others. Wonder if she's a Zivah Zahav follower.

Chimes…

We're going to get hit hard at home. Mom's and my earnings are supposed to help supplement Dad's erratic income as a consultant. Her new business, Domestic Goddess, hasn't taken off as expected. Baking and herbal essential oils will go only so far if you depend on word-of-mouth referrals. She hates bringing attention to herself through marketing and advertising. That may have to change after today.

"Guys, I suspect this is just the beginning. The WLC will eventually get their claws on all our affairs," Josef states.

That's an interesting comment coming from him. The WLC can't come after the two of them. They're fortunate within their misfortune, they must have barely any money at all. My thoughts jump as an awful feeling takes over me. "Dahvid Toledano— did you know about this?" I demand.

Bleep…!

Uncalled for. Horribly rude. Apologize!

Jazz gasps and covers her mouth, as if she had been the one to make the accusation. Dahvid's expression divulges how deeply offended he is.

"Dahvid, I can't believe I said that, please forgive me. What I meant to ask was if your group speculated that this could happen."

Chimes…

As he prepares to answer, I'm realizing that too much sugar and not enough protein for breakfast is not a good idea, not good at all. I'm crashing big time.

Dahvid looks up with a frown and responds, "Ms. Stafford, this is scary and upsetting for all of us. To answer your question, no— I did not know, but it does not come as a surprise. The World Chancellor is known to be spectacularly cruel and greedy. He is an expert at targeting the vulnerable. He will stop at nothing until he takes over and reverses time!"

"And just as we're trying to speed things up," Tomas quips unintentionally.

Josef jumps in, "They're starting with highly philanthropic, well-known people to create a panic."

"Taking over our businesses the day we get deactivated is a strategically brilliant move. My paternal unit has the same way of thinking. Hit them when they're down, it's such a cowardly way of being. The damage this kind of person can do is… unspeakably malevolent," Tomas decides to share.

"I'm so sorry you've had to experience this firsthand. It took a lot of courage to share that with us," Jazz remarks.

I'm stunned. I can't believe it. Tomas has had to deal with this type of behavior within his own family— his whole life? He's never said a word about it to me.

Bleep!

Not about you.

I feel so guilty. "Tomas, I'm so sorry…"

Chimes…

Josef is noticeably uncomfortable. "Sahrit, does the document have a deadline as to when they'll be contacting you to take over?"

The question makes her start crying all over again. "Is… ASAP… a deadline?"

"We will get this resolved, I promise," Dahvid

states. "I have contacted a specialist in Youth Corporate Law, for guidance. His office is in Scarsdale, on the first floor of Garth Manor. Anyone familiar with that location?"

"You know I am— it's the same high-rise complex we live in," Tomas replies. "If I need him, I won't have to travel far."

"You live in one of those fancy buildings?" I exclaim. How can it be that I know nothing about him, nothing at all? My thoughts shift to the millions of kids that I know nothing about either but depend on me. "Jazz, we need to be on top of Liberty World, it's going to explode any second now!"

"On it! I've set up extra measures to block any outside interference. Sahrit and I are adding resources and suggestions on how to manage stress and anxiety," Jazz replies.

"Thank you, Ms. Ross and Ms. Bana, you..." I stop cold, the announcement begins:

ATTENTION HYBRIDS WORLDWIDE
AGES 8 - 18
MANDATORY DEACTIVATION
MARCH 4 - 8, 2041
PRE-REGISTRATION REQUIRED

Check listings for locations
and times of operation.
No discomfort. No down time.

Immediately after, this shows up:

BREAKING NEWS

Expecting large crowds
Recalibration Centers
transformed into
Deactivation Centers.
Additional buildings erected.

The screen resumes its normal appearance and Dahvid springs into action, "Everyone—we are ending the meeting. Register ASAP to be part of the first wave. Stay focused, obey instructions, remain vigilant, be careful. Later."

My panicked breathing patterns affect the spheres graceful movements. Eucalyptus blows in, I inhale— deeply. Maarlee's golden pineapple sphere appears. "We need to talk ASAP if not sooner! MM."

"Can't— Later, JS," I reply. How could I be so dismissive with her? But what else could I do? I'm feeling queasy, the mega adrenaline rush consumed the rest of my carb-filled breakfast. I better eat a couple of protein bars before we go. I sit on the bed and watch real time images of the newly transformed Recalibration Centers. They're surrounded by the same menacing ilk of bullies as the ones yesterday at the WLC. Their message is clear— don't mess with us. We reserve the right to mess with you.

They hate us, we hate them.

"Go ahead, Intelly, Bleep! me, change colors, do something! Are you still with me? Will you still be with me after?" I yell out. "Will you ever do your thing for me, again?" I start throwing pillows all over the floor and then throw myself, face down, on the bed. Without looking at the screen, I know Jazz wants to get in touch; the scent of jasmine puffs in with a soft little 'plink' sound.

She must have seen my deep dive into despair. I turn over and force myself to sit up.

"Hey…" she sighs, "got a minute? I have a special request."

"I don't have the energy to produce a single second," I reply, sniffling.

"I'd… like to apply… to be on your Imaginarian Team."

"The whaat?" I snap back, wiping my teary face with the bed sheet.

"You know… The job you offered Becca and Sammie at The WLC?"

I flash back to how that helped the two very upset sisters. "Oh, yeah— that. All Josef's idea. Can't take credit."

Chimes…

"I'd like to interview for the position by

extending an invitation to a very special event today. Would you care to join me?"

"Special event— today? Did you already forget where we're going?" I snap back, again.

Jazz starts whispering, "Of course not, silly! How could I? Play along— please. Sy's awake. He'll be in here any second. My goal is to put a positive spin on today's impending nightmare. I need to get us all through it."

"Got it— I'm listening…"

She goes back to her normal volume. "Are you aware that the New York Philharmonic was founded almost two hundred years ago?"

"Gee… how did that important fact ever slip my mind!" I respond sarcastically.

"I mention this because in preparation of their bicentennial celebration next year, some of the musicians will be displaying instruments outside a brand new venue. We need to reserve a spot because it'll be packed. There's also a surprise performance indoors. They'll be demonstrating how to play a new instrument never seen or heard before. Exciting… right?"

"Sounds amazing!" I'm stunned by her ability to create such an elaborate story in such a short amount of time.

She adds, "Can't wait to see the tablescapes, either, bet they'll have gorgeous place settings and floral centerpieces. Maybe, if we're lucky, we can each bring one home as souvenirs." By now we're both at the window looking at each other, smiling and waving.

"Let's show our brothers how much they're loved by bringing them along for a double date," Jazz suggests.

"Normally, I wouldn't consider walking to the corner with Jake, let alone asking him out on date, but in this case…"

Jazz giggles her cute giggle at my sarcastic, brotherly-love remark. Hmmm… Using imagination and humor really helps deflect anger and anxiety.

Chimes…

"Greetings from Nebula Eight," raspy voiced, little Sy announces, standing next to his sister. He's ready to go, dressed in a superhero costume, mask and all.

I reach over for my wand, still on the bed from last night and proclaim, "*Mademoiselle Rossé*, for your improvisational gifts and stellar ability to share joy by seeing everything through rose-colored glasses, I dub thee Mastermind Imaginarian Extraordinaire."

"What about me? What about me?"

"Sir Symon Ross, I dub thee, Supreme Defender Of All Galaxies." Jazz bows like a ballerina, and he like a courtly prince. The auto control shade lowers on cue. Five minutes later, her sphere comes back. "Jess… can you hear me?" she's whispering again, sounding shaky.

"Yes… What's wrong?"

"I don't want Sy to hear me say this… I'm really scared, just like you are. No amount of yoga or meditation could make a dent. My poor little brother has been through so much trauma already, and he's barely eight and now this? Thanks for playing along, keep it going while he's with us. Okay?" Jazz says through her bunny rabbit sniffles.

"I'm— more than scared but I'll give it my best shot. I can't vouch for Jake the Jock."

"Good luck coercing your date… I know! Ask him to do it for Sy." Her sphere drifts away, leaving a trail of tiny little flowers in its path.

I walk through our shared bathroom and knock on Jake's door, he growls a response, "Whatever you're sellin' I ain't buyin'…"

"It's important Jake… "

"Go away, Squirt…"

"I need to come in!"

"Fine— in!" he groans in defeat.

Since he decided to remodel his bedroom

yesterday, Dad had to board up his one and only window. The ambiance is that of ten stinky lockers. "Yuuuck!" I blurt out, holding my nose. "This is disgusting!" I walk through piles of stuff towards his door that opens to the hallway. I step onto the edge of his bed to turn on the ceiling fan. Air circulation is badly needed. I pull on the broken chain and socks fly off the blades like dusty projectiles.

"Jazz and I are going on a walk in fifteen. She's bringing Sy and lucky me— I get to bring you!" I say with fake enthusiasm.

"Don't give me the girlie pink lemonade and cupcake version. I heard what's going on, and where you want to go. No! Out! I don't need you micromanaging my every move, Ms. Big Shot. Back off!" he barks.

Trying to keep my cool, I respond, "Don't do it for me, do it for Sy. Do you have any idea how much he looks up to you and misses you? It's been so long…"

"He does?" Jake speaks into the pillow.

"You know he does, so get up, get registered and freshen up. We're meeting them outside in fifteen. Move it!" Jazz was right on target, a dash of emotional manipulation never hurts to get a point across.

His arm falls out to the side which is my clue to pull on it. We used to do that when we were little. He'd make me think I was stronger than he was. Despite his larger size, he'd tumble out of bed. Right now, I am stronger so he lands on the floor, wearing yesterday's crumpled, stinky clothes. "Great— just great — you're a mess, Jake. Ughh— you reek of smoke and alcohol!"

He gets up and heads towards me like a crazed animal. I freak out and hop backwards, expecting to escape through the hallway. Instead, I bump the back of my head on the door frame. He laughs and takes a swing at me but misses. He splatters the wall with red.

"You're acting like a maniac and now you've busted your knuckle!" I yell out, rushing into the bathroom for the first aid kit.

"Another hole, Mom and Dad will be beyond absolutely thrilled at your handy work," I say, bandaging his hand. It's been over a year since Jake and I've had some time, alone. Too bad this episode involves alcohol-induced rage and bloodshed.

"Go shower and keep your fist dry!"

He growls, grunts and curses.

"You should be more grateful, considering I left a few scraps of food. You better hide your hand from Mom, or she'll ask you questions you won't want to answer."

"Like what?" he asks, trying to come out of his

mental fog.

"Like, where were you last night?"

"Oh, yeah… that. I was at a meeting. We're planning another revolt."

"Whaaat? Have you lost the last neuron that was hiding in the recesses of your brain? This is the last thing I needed to deal with today." I walk out into the hallway and look down from the top of the stairs. Mom's sitting on the sofa, she seems very worried. Halfway down, I notice Dad's office door is completely closed. Not a good sign, not good at all.

Mom looks up and demands to know what just happened. I explain that it was the usual. "Jake's mad because I woke him up too early."

"Why did you wake him up? He was cramming for exams and stayed up late last night." Mom assures me.

"I'm sure… that was it," I remark.

"Jesse Girl, this morning was so pleasant. Now that he's awake— he'll be acting like an enraged bull."

"Tell me about it…" I say, rubbing my head.

"Where are you going?" she asks.

"Jazz has invited us to attend the event of a lifetime!"

"Really? What is it?" Mom's mood shifts.

"It's an Implant Farewell Party sponsored by the New York Philharmonic. Everyone that's anyone, age eight to eighteen, is expected to attend the gala."

"Whaaat? So soon?" Mom jumps to her feet.

"Yup! Just found out. We want to avoid the long lines. The four of us are going."

"This is terrible, horrible— please be careful, no confrontations!" Mom implores.

"No problem, the buildings are covered with armed guards," I explain, reassuringly.

Jake clunks hard on every creaky step, on his way down. That large, hard head of his must weigh even more when it's wet. He grunts a good morning, but doesn't dare look at Mom.

"Nice cologne, Jake," she says, as he walks by her. "Whew… too much," she mouths, waving her hand by her nose.

He grabs some fruit and a couple of energy bars. Surprisingly, he remembers to stuff them into his left pocket while he keeps his right hand hidden.

"What's with your right hand, Jake? Are you hiding something?"

"No, Mom… nothing. It's part of Coach Calloway's new sports training. Use your other hand to make it stronger kind-of-thing," he responds.

Such an amateur. What a stupid answer—
even for him. By Mom's expression, I can tell
she doesn't believe his lie, but right now she's
worried about bigger things. She walks us to
the door and waves goodbye.

Sy spots us immediately from across the street
and shrills with delight. He rolls down their hill,
stopping just short of the curb. He stands up,
looks both ways and crosses the street. The
agile little boy jumps into Jake's arms and
coaxes him into performing one of their famous
acrobatic acts.

"Bear, throw me up in the air! Throw me, throw
me!" Jake does as he's told, and his bad mood
disappears in a snap. The only person on the
planet who can soften Jake Stafford's heart is
Sweet Sy. They couldn't be more opposite:
Jake is an immature, big burly block of a guy
while Sy is a sweet, very wise, wisp of a boy.
Before he was adopted by the Rosses, their
son lived in an Ethiopian orphanage, where he
suffered from awful neglect and malnutrition.
According to docs, proper care and hormonal
treatments will help him catch up.

I cross the street to join Jazz. "So nice that
we're going to see the new building together,"
she says cheerfully.

Our walk begins and she comments, "Can you

believe that they finished the venue last night just in time for today's grand performance?"

"But I thought…" Jake attempts to correct Jazz. I shake my head. He gets the signal. My brother is not the brightest star in the sky, but he knows that we have to keep our comments and emotions in check for Sy. Jazz asks her little brother to describe what he thinks the new building looks like. His elaborate description of an extra-terrestrial habitat is a welcomed distraction during the rest of our brisk morning walk.

"There it is!" Sy exclaims with excitement, "I see it! I see the musicians holding their big instruments, too!"

Since we're the first ones to show up, we're way outnumbered by soldiers— I mean musicians. Sy's enormous deep, blue-ocean eyes are taking it all in. Big, burly guards wearing uniforms are in a menacing stance, holding their heavy weapons, better suited for active combat in a foreign war zone. But, they must be prepared because us Hybrids are such a violent bunch… Grrr…

As we get closer to the entrance, Sy senses our anxiety. Even though he's holding his sister's hand, he reaches for mine, too. Maybe someday I'll be able to tell him how grateful I am that he's holding my hand on such a scary, horrible day. Jake decides to wait outside, needing to enter on his own terms— I get that.

Jazz whispers something in Sy's ear; he lets go of me. A guard outside instructs us to show our devices, displaying our name and confirmation number. He takes Intelly from me and places it in a pre-labeled, self-closing bag. I hope they plan on returning it when we leave. Hope our personalities are left intact when we leave, too. He points at the entrance.

"Follow me," I say bravely, leading the way. Everything inside has been carefully planned and meticulously arranged. It smells like institutional disinfectant, and it's colder than it is outside. Sy is enjoying playing with the steam of his breath inside this enormous refrigerator. Even though there aren't any windows, the overhead lights make it unbearably bright. I place my hand over my eyes like a visor to create shade, so I can see where we're going. Black and yellow striped arrows on the floor point towards the back, where they've arranged twelve long narrow tables with stainless steel tops. The lab-like tables are running parallel to the back wall, creating a familiar, gray, snake-like formation. There are four heavy metal chairs per table, two for us Hybrids to sit side by side, as we face our implant executioners. We're split up. Jazz and Sy end up on the opposite side of the room. We're ordered not to sit yet, as we stand behind our assigned chairs.

Today's parade of attendants is dressed in white uniforms, shielded helmets, gloves and shoe protectors. I panic— we're having a surgical procedure done in front of others? Will they at least cover our eyes or give us anesthesia to knock us out, while the implants are deactivated? I feel like screaming and running out the door. If only I could do my breathing exercises, but in this temperature, the steam would attract too much attention. I focus on the large squared-off medical cases each tech is carrying. I imagine them as giant emeralds.

They're placed in unison on the stainless steel tabletops, with military precision. They make a single, well-rehearsed, metal to metal sound that echoes throughout the building.

My implant executioner stands in front of me and indicates with its hands to sit. The person points over its shoulder at the image on the wall behind, illustrating how far back to push our sleeves. We have to expose four fingers worth from where the hand meets the arm. I nervously rest my exposed wrists, veins up, on the cold metal surface.

"This won't hurt," I hear a woman's voice whisper through the helmet. She scans my left wrist and says, "Jessica Stafford, age 14, address 37 Anderson Ave. Scarsdale, NY. Correct?"

"Correct." My voice is so shaky.

She points at my right wrist and pulls out a metallic cylindrical tube from the case. She presses it against my skin. I feel intense heat but no pain. A yellow band, a half inch wide, starts appearing on my left wrist and a red one on my right. Oh please, no, not red— not now. My body starts shaking uncontrollably. The woman behind the mask looks at me intently, tears are forming in her eyes, she whispers, "Silence, Light and Beauty." She then points at a sign explaining that wrists must remain dry and covered, no exposure to light and no physical exertion for twenty-four hours. The bands will disappear on their own, after that, life as usual. Yeah— right!

I look at the lab tech intently, wondering why she said, "Silence, Light and Beauty." Why do those words sound so familiar? My mind is in a fog. Her eyebrows come together, as she motions me to get up so the next kid can sit.

As I turn away, towards the front, it hits me… the attendant is Mrs. García! She used the title of my essay to let me know it was her. The WLC must have recruited key, quality people accustomed to working with kids to do their dirty work. I sure hope no one heard her speak to me. Hope to see her again…

I just felt empathy— where are my Chimes? There's nothing! Where's the reserve? Oh noo— Josef was right, we're totally, completely, absolutely disconnected. Don't panic. Keep walking. Don't cry. Don't faint. Breathe.

I pass a multitude of frozen, scared faces, waiting their turn. I feel as hollow as the sound of my footsteps echoing from the cold, concrete floor to the flat, white, prefab walls onto the steel ceiling and back down again. Watching the steam of my breath, I wonder if that's all that's left of me.

The guard's gloved hand returns my Intellitela still inside the bag with the WLC logo on it. How thrilling… we did get a souvenir to remember this special day. A close second to getting an imaginary floral centerpiece.

Outside, double lines are wrapping around the building. I'm instructed to wait behind the barricade for the rest of my group. Feeling numb from the experience, I search for a little patch of winter sunlight to stand under.

"There she is!" Sy exclaims, pointing at me with excitement. Wonder what he thinks just happened. He's such a happy boy, look at him, marveling at the shadows made by bare tree branches. Jazz and I look at each other, teary-eyed, with nothing to say. Jake comes out of the building, looking alert instead of his typical tussled, spaced-out, clunky self. Did the disconnection turn him into a human being, or did the experience just sober him up? I wave and call out, "Bear… Over here!"

Sy reaches for his sister's hand, Jake offers me his. I take it and squeeze on it, gently. The four of us begin our journey back home.

"There's Tomas Kesher and Madison Kesher!" Sy exclaims, as we see them walk towards us.

"Hiii, Jake Stafford," Maddy says, melodiously, flashing a warm smile and twirling a strand of wavy golden-brown hair.

"Hey…" he responds shyly, raising his right hand.

Tomas becomes agitated by the sight of the bandage, "Did they do surgery on you? What exactly do they do to you? Does it hurt?"

"Nah… don't sweat it, man. This is from a recent athletic injury," he brags.

"Hope you're well enough to play at the game next week. I'll make sure to be there and cheer you on," Maddy offers flirtatiously.

We walk away, and Jake speaks out, "Well, well, well, what-da-ya know— I thought she couldn't stand me."

"D'you like her?" Jazz wonders.

"Well, yeahhh! Look at her, who wouldn't?"

"Tell her next time," Sy suggests.

"Hmm… thank you Little Man, I might just do that," Jake replies, grinning ear to ear.

Lost in four very different worlds, we make it back in silence and split up without a word. Jazz and Sy walk up their steps slowly, standing in front of their amethyst door, under the floating roofline.

"Look at them. Aren't they just beautiful?" I whisper to Jake as light rain begins to fall.

We watch Jazz bend over and says something to Sy. He smiles and nods, enthusiastically. Still holding hands, they take a couple of steps beyond the overhang and face skyward. Jazz, in her brilliance, figured out how to cope with her feelings. Her tears are blending with the rain. If only it was that easy to wash away our fears and our rage.

Jake pulls out his Intellitela. I'm hoping he's going to capture the touching moment across the street, instead he says, "Touchdown!"

"Football at a time like this?" I remark, looking over at his device. The screen is frozen.

INTERNATIONAL BREAKING NEWS
Riots Erupt In Deactivation Centers.
Mobs of raging Hybrids attack WLC guards.
Shots fired. Stampedes. Chaos.
Multiple injuries, possible loss of life.

"This is terrible! This is horrible! I can't take it anymore!" I yell out. "Could things get any worse?" I'm shaking, too furious to cry.

"They could've been a whole lot worse, trust me. The coordination was off."

"Whaat?"

"I… was supposed to be in charge of coordinating the signals worldwide so the riots would erupt simultaneously. Leaders wanted one big, worldwide ka-boom!"

We're interrupted by thunder and then I say, "You? In charge? How could you accept such a thing?" With rain pouring down, I grab him by the arms, as if tiny me could shake an ounce of sense into his dense brain.

"Hear me out, will you? While you and Jazz were talking, I realized I had to buy time and think things through. You came in to rush me. I wasn't with it enough to figure out how to get us out of a dangerous situation. I freaked out and when that happens— I act like a madman," he explains.

"Sounds like you're freaked out a lot, lately."

"Aren't you?" he replies.

"Why did you wait outside The Center?" I yell, over the loud rain.

"I stayed outside as long as I could, I was

contacting people, trying to talk them out of today's plans. Turns out a bunch had already chickened out, others must have overslept and didn't answer— bunch of slackers. The guards were keeping an eye on me. They were starting to suspect something was up. I walked by them, pretending I was talking to Mom. Then I went inside."

"Brilliant move, Jake Stafford, now the guards have fully identified you. At least those slacker friends of yours had enough sense not to get sucked in by peer pressure and backed out. People were injured or they've died— and for what?"

"I'm always furious about something, we both are. Do you ever wonder why?"

"I do," I mumble.

"You've found ways of channeling it. I want mine. The plan made sense, especially after drinking for hours with a bunch of guys."

"You've got to stop getting involved with violent groups, it doesn't lead to anything."

"No problem, guessing by now they've suspended my lifetime membership."

"Don't be so sure, Mom and Dad can't go through anymore of this, nor can I." I grab him by the arms again and say, "Jake, listen to me. If you would take the time to read up on history, you'll find that riots have never solved anything. And still— people are willing to die for a cause or kill others for it. You want to learn how to fight?"

"Wanna teach me how to fight like a girl?"

"I'll teach you how to fight intelligently and protest effectively— with words. Seen my collection of trophies, lately?"

Jake guides me towards our front door, we sit on our wet step and he puts his arm around me. Through soaking hoods, our heads touch. I've missed my big brother taking care of me. Sounds like I'll be taking care of him now. Hope it's not too late. "Where've you been, Bear? I don't recognize you anymore."

"I'm sixteen," he replies without letting go. The rain ends and so does our moment.

"Moom, Daad," I call out as we walk inside. Jake clonks back upstairs but not without throwing his drenched jacket overboard for me to catch. His bedroom door closes gently, for a change.

Dad calls out from his office, "Jess, are you both okay?"

"Yes, Dad, okay, no local riots or physical pain to report." I take our wet jackets and boots and put them back outside.

"Come in for a few minutes— we need to have

a serious talk." He sounds really upset. Why is he wanting to talk to me? Jake should be the one on trial. After all, he's the one that added a new edition to his Wall of Shame.

"Yes, sir?" He turns around in his creaky chair and studies me carefully. I'm soaking wet and shivering.

He hesitates, "…Never mind, we'll talk later."

What a relief. I start turning around but reconsider, "Can I ask you something, Dad?"

"Is it important?" Dad asks, now sounding rushed for time.

"I think it is," I reply, pulling off my wet knit cap and gloves.

"Why is it that every time we're close to getting something done, it falls apart? It's infuriating!" I say, tossing my stuff to the floor in frustration. He points at the chair for me to sit. "We've been working so hard to do what we were expected to do, and we're just faced with obstacles. The irony of it all is that they're being created by the very ones who wanted us to be superhuman in the first place! I feel lots of stuff gurgling inside me, like soda."

"Say more about that," Dad requests.

"We were so close to getting the right to vote at fourteen, and then— nothing, it's gone, not even discussed. It's like it never happened.

And now, after today, all our hard work to learn how to live with the implants— all the things we've planned on doing— literally zapped in an instant!" Hot tears roll down my face. I take off my heavy sweater and drop it in the floor.

Dad leans over and picks it up and holds it in his arms like a baby. He looks very sad. "I know how you must feel," he responds, softly.

"No Dad! I don't think you can....!" I snap. "What're we supposed to do now, huh? Just sit around and watch the world burn, get blown away, collapse or fall into the ocean? You know we're at that point…?"

Dad looks down, as if taking all the blame. "We had hoped, as nano tech designers, to create a secure path for you and future generations. In retrospect, we failed you miserably. We should've paid more attention and fought harder. It's been so many years, and yet…" Dad turns away to face the garden. "I'm not convinced we'll ever fully recover from the human devastation on this ailing planet," Dad starts crying and reaches for a tissue. "You better go talk to your mother now, she's in the backyard."

"But we're not finished…"

Without turning back around, he hands me the sweater over his shoulder. Feeling useless and worthless, I step over my drenched cap and gloves and walk out. I put the sweater back on with Dad's warmth still in it. I force myself to go outside for round two.

"Mooom?" I call out before stepping outside.

"I'm over heeere… around the baaack," she responds.

Using an old rag, she's wiping off the last of the rain from the dilapidated wood swing. We have to position ourselves on it in a certain way, otherwise the rusted chains pop off, on one side or the other.

"One, two, and…" Mom recites.

"Mom… Dad is very upset."

 "How upset?"

"Crying-with-a-tissue upset?" I reply. "I wanted to stay and talk, but he told me to come and see you. What's going on, Mom?"

"He's not great in the emotional department. Sound familiar?" She pauses and changes the subject. "Remember when we used to sit like this when you were just a bud of a leaf? We'd invent crazy, fun stories together?"

"I do and loved every minute," I reply.

"We've always wanted to give you every opportunity to express yourself, your feelings, doubts, questions about the world. You've always been so aware of everything…"

I just had an epiphany— thanks to Mom, I became a skilled and confident speaker. But, it might also be how I became a skilled and confident liar. I feel a big knot forming in my throat and in the pit of my stomach.

She takes a deep breath and gets up, but just enough to change position, otherwise she'd catapult me into outer space. That would be a great way of escaping from whatever's coming. I'm amused by the thought. She looks very serious now that her whole body is towards me. "We love that you're so devoted to your causes and to your fans on Liberty World, but there are limits…"

She's starting to cry, too?

"Jess… when you walked out of here yesterday, you told us you were going to meet Josef at the village."

"I did go to the village!" I answer, defensively.

Mom continues, "But… you also went to the WLC behind our backs!" She raises her voice.

"Mom— I…"

"No! I don't want to hear any outlandish stories or excuses this time. You're going to hear what I have to say. Understood?"

"Yes, ma'am." I've never seen her like this.

She explains that she and Dad are upset

because they asked me specifically not to stir up trouble.

"Bunch of liars!" I blurt out and quickly cover my mouth.

"Jessica Lynn Stafford!"

"No, sorry, not you! I just realized that they lied about the deactivation process. It does have side effects. I'm feeling queasy and dizzy." I'm starting to shake and cry.

Mom's upset shifts to concern. She can tell I'm going into full anxiety attack mode. She asks permission to hug me.

"Breathe… I'm right here."

"Emeraaald?" I call out, "Where are you? I have nothing left, Mom, nothing!" I sob.

Mom starts running her fingers up and down my back and arms, simulating body brushing, reminding me Emerald is always available.

"I was so scared… I tried not to show it. Even if… they took our devices… at the door. I imagined that the surgical cases… on the stainless tables… were giant emeralds."

I'm hyperventilating so she keeps brushing. "You're very brave and very resourceful, My Jesse Girl. Stop talking and do three second inhales and exhales."

I close my eyes, do as I'm told for a change,

and focus on my body sensations. Based on my breathing patterns, Mom knows when I can stop.

"Want to try my latest mix?" she asks warmly.

I nod and watch her reach into her jacket's pocket and pull out a small clear bottle with a dark green cap. She flips the top open with her thumb and places it under my nose.

Inhaling the heavenly aroma makes me say, "Now that's intense— I love it! What is it? It smells… emerald. Is that possible?"

"Essentially, yes." Mom giggles at her own pun.

"What's in it?"

"It's my private label. See, no name yet." She points at the little blank sticker. "It has a touch of rosemary, some lemongrass, lavender and, of course, eucalyptus, I can't divulge the rest… I've been sworn to secrecy by the EOA."

I rest my head on her shoulder. "What's the EOA, Mommy?"

"Essential Oil Agency," Mom chuckles and kisses my head, tenderly, three times.

Now that I'm feeling calmer, she asks again why I went to the WLC yesterday without permission. I explain that originally, I hadn't planned on it. I'd been alerted about the last two available seats, so I took it as a sign. I was forced to make a snap decision.

"Really? Who forced you?"

"No one… it was all in my head. I thought of nothing else, other than I had to be there. Josef wasn't thrilled about it either, believe me. I'm not proud of what I did."

"Glad you recognize it," Mom responds sternly.

"Going without asking you was not a good move— all right— a terrible move. What's worse is that I used the pouty-puppy thing to get Josef to agree to come with me."

Mom shakes her head, putting her hands on her cheeks, trying hard not to smile. "I'll never forgive myself for teaching you that."

I explain that it's a great tool. Josef stayed with me the whole time. He said he owed it to both of them to escort me safely.

"Such a fine young man, wish he and Jake could be friends…" Mom sighs deeply.

"Face it, Mom, they couldn't be more opposite."

"Back to the WLC…" Mom reminds me.

"It was much more upsetting than I expected. We needed to see what The Chancellor was blocking from the feed yesterday morning."

"What feed yesterday morning?" Mom wonders.

Whoa... Mom just confirmed my suspicion, adults didn't know about The Chancellor's Grand Performance. I try to explain to her what we saw but keep losing it. It's hard to talk about the part about the dignitary getting carried off the stage and the girl who fainted on the floor. Mom cradles me as I sob.

"Oh, Sweetheart, it sounds awful... just imagine how concerned we were, when we found out you were there."

I straighten up and ask, "How did you find out, anyway?"

"By watching the news feed at the top of the hour. We were worried sick you'd fall victim to another media frenzy. On top of that, we felt deceived. Can you understand why we're so upset?"

"I do, and I'm sooo sorry. It's crazy that I didn't think about letting you know or worried about being seen or anything. How stupid can I get? When will I ever learn not to act on impulse?"

"In theory, as you mature, but there's no guarantee of that."

I ask her if she thinks Jazz's friends are Hybrid spies. Mom reassures me that they're nice girls, she knows their parents well. I'm also congratulated for yet another outlandish story.

"Did you say anything to Josef that could have

gotten you noticed?" Mom asks.

"I didn't say much of anything. Wait— I did, once… no— twice, well actually, several times. Someone kept shushing me."

"Someone marked you, My Sweet, it's an old trick. Reporters use their night vision to find people in dark venues. They must have identified you and alerted the media outlets."

"How in the world do you know about this kind of stuff?"

"Umm… let's just say I get around," she explains, as she opens her small vial again. I watch her rub some of the oil inside her wrists and then inhale it, eyes closed.

"While you were on your way back to Scarsdale, the media showed clips of what happened at the debate last year. They claim that you and your Hybrid followers were the original instigators responsible for organizing the violent revolt that got Jake arrested. They warned parents not to let children out of our sight for an instant! Ludicrous, isn't it?"

If she only knew that suspecting us isn't ludicrous at all. Her own daughter is part of something big, really big, that will overthrow The World Chancellor's regime.

"We didn't want to believe you were there, but there was a clip of you leaving the building, so it was undeniable."

"How did you know it wasn't an old clip?"

"Because Becca's parents called, saying how grateful they were that you and Josef were sitting next to their girls. We got very concerned and tried getting ahold of you and couldn't. Tell me the truth, did you disconnect your device?"

"No— I promise! The lines of communication were blocked by The Chancellor in the morning and then they got overloaded after the meeting at The WLC. We were having all kinds of trouble."

Mom continues, "I thought we had agreed to stay out of the public eye— and yet here we are— *déjà vous* all over again…"

"You're right. What if they start ridiculing me again? I'm still getting over all of that. Remember that cartoon of me looking like a measuring stick with long, stringy hair on it, and…" I start crying again.

"My heart hurts just thinking about it, Sweetie. When you become a parent, you'll understand that anything that happens to you, happens to us. So for all our sakes, let's not tempt fate." She hands me the tiny bottle. "Do you want to rub on some of my new magic potion?"

"Can't. Our wrists have to stay dry and not exposed to light for 24 hours."

"What kind of surgical instruments did they use on you? Did they hurt you in any way?" She starts crying. "Oh, my poor babies."

"I only used the term surgical for a dramatical effect. It was all done with scanners and some sort of small, metal cylinder."

Mom sighs with relief. She pulls her thick, long dark hair away from her face. It looks like when heavy theatre curtains part, as the performance is about to begin.

She speaks softly, "Jess, you might as well hear it from me…"

Oh, no, I knew it! My parents are getting a divorce and all because of me and Jake! That's what Dad really wanted to tell me, but he didn't want me to feel guilty. She takes my hands. "This may come as a total surprise to you, but… at one point in my life, I was a highly rebellious and expressive teenager. I'd sneak out through my bedroom window."

"You whaaat?" I exclaim.

She gestures to keep it down and continues, "You name it, I was there, protesting for the rights of the downtrodden, compelled to fight injustice. I was convinced that, if I made enough of a fuss, I'd somehow be heard, and it would all get resolved." Mom gives me some examples, but no matter how hard I try to listen, I find nothing to explain why they're getting divorced. "Eventually, in one of my trips to juvenile court…"

"Whaaat? You went to court?"

"The last time I was taken in, my case was assigned to a judge who knew my parents. She gave me an ultimatum that saved my life. I was warned that if I showed up again, she'd lock me up and throw away the key."

"You were going to go to jail? Youuu?"

"At the time, it would have been juvenile detention but eventually, yes— at the rate I was going. The next day, the judge arranged for a visit at a woman's penitentiary. That did it, I stopped getting in trouble, just like that!" she says, snapping her fingers. "It had never occurred to me that there could be negative consequences, if actions were for the good."

"That's really deep, Mom…" My mind wonders away thinking that, maybe, Dad found out she had shot somebody at a riot.

"Jess, I'm speaking. Are you listening to me? There's a point to this."

"Yes, I am," I half lie.

"There's so much of me, in both of you and Jake. That's why we refer to you as our little apples. You know, the ones that don't fall far from the tree?" She forces a weak smile.

"I thought it was just a cute nickname."

Mom goes from being momentarily enchanted to very serious. "So… to conclude… if you think I minimize everything or seem to live in denial, believe me, young lady, I'm not. I do it because everything triggers me. I want to get involved and fix it all. It's like a drug…"

"Really? Even after so many years?"

"Really— addiction is addiction, mine was to the adrenaline rush, it never goes away. It's taken a lot of work and discipline to overcome. The gardening, the herbal mixes, cooking, baking, all keep me very busy— on purpose."

A rush of something— not adrenaline, surges through me, and I start laughing.

"Really? Are you that insensitive that you're laughing at something so personal that was so difficult to share?"

Mom loses her cool. My laughing stops.

"Mom, no, sorry, I'm not making fun of you, on the contrary. What you're telling me is beyond absolutely fantabulous! I'm laughing, because I'm thrilled!"

"Whaaat?"

"You have no idea how long I've wished you had a secret past and you do! You really do!"

Mom ignores her own tears. "Seriously?"

"Yes! You were just too perfect. But now, I recognize myself in you!" I tell her about my crazy fantasies, their impending divorce because she shot someone.

"I don't know if I should laugh or cry. Where world would you come up with something so outlandish? Never mind… silly question." She pauses to take another whiff of her potion. "What I just shared with you is private. Do not tell Jake— I mean it! You hear me? We have to handle things differently with him."

"I won't, Mom, promise. Does anyone else know? Does Dad?"

"Yes, of course Dad knows. When you're married you don't keep secrets from each other. Daniela Ross, Jazz's mom knows because she's my attorney. I had to confide in her last year… I was worried my past would catch up with us during 'The Incident' and the media would hurt you even more."

I lean over and give Mom the biggest hug ever. Crack! Snap! Those sounds can only mean one thing and one thing only.

Flomp! We land on the saturated ground, our ancient, rotted swing gave way— finally!

"That's what happens when you have a heavy conversation with your teenaged daughter," Mom remarks.

I just realized that our laughter is one of the many things we have in common. I have a new appreciation for genetics.

Reaching for a fallen tree branch next to me, I lift it like a sword in battle. "Today the swing… tomorrow the bed!" I proclaim. "Ouch! Ouch!" Horrible burning pain shoots through my left arm. Mom helps me lower it slowly. "I hate being constantly reminded. Do you think my arm will ever heal?"

"Let's talk about that some other time." There's an odd look in her eyes. It must be that she's afraid to tell me that it's permanently damaged. I don't want to know, I've had enough incoming data for one day. I take a breath and say, "Thank you for trusting me with your story, Mom. Will you forgive me for not thinking and being highly irresponsible?"

"Let me get this straight: you want me— to forgive you— for being— just like me?" We burst out laughing again.

"I love you so much, Mommy."

"I'm crazy about you, my Little Apple. Now come in for a snack and then go lie down. Rest is the only remedy for the overall exhaustion you'll be feeling soon."

Mom helps me get up off of the ground, so I don't put pressure on my wrists. We hold each other's muddy hands and swing them on our way back to the side kitchen entrance. We let go so she can remove her sloppy boots, leaving them outside to dry. She guides me towards the sink and runs warm water over my hands, rinsing off the dirt, very gently. No wonder herbs and flowers do so well under her care.

Before I go upstairs, Mom requests one last thing. "Please, think of the impact of your actions on others. Take it from me, your-not-as-boring-as-you-thought-I-once-was Mom."

I blow her a kiss wishing I could agree with her, but I can't. I don't know what I'm about to get us into. I offer to look in on Jake.

I push his door open in such a way that it doesn't make that old haunted house creaky sound. Look at that… all 200 pounds of him—fast asleep. All that's visible is a tuft of wavy, light brown hair which earned him my nickname, Teddy Bear. I sure miss those days when we used to talk about anything and everything, late into the night. We'd leave the bathroom doors open between our rooms. How naive to think our parents could be fooled into thinking we were fast asleep. How were we to know that they could hear us through the air vents and under the doors? When Jake the Jock hit sixteen, everything changed. The talkative, inquisitive part of him must have been extracted by intergalactic travelers. Before closing his door, I whisper, "I've missed you, Bear."

"Me too, Leaf," he replies, covering the rest of his head.

I walk into my room, thrilled he called me Leaf. Sitting on the edge of my bed, legs dangling, I collapse backwards from exhaustion. Intelly picks up on my needs, lowers the shades and dims the lights. A whiff of Mom's new custom mix presents itself. Before my eyes close completely, I make sure the spheres haven't lost their graceful flow after such a stressful morning. As awful as today was, it served to resuscitate my connection with Jake. I was afraid it was gone but it's just been dormant.

TOWERS
ACT VIII

🌏 **Monday, March 4, 2041 3:30 PM**

My eyes open to Sahrit's melodious voice playing in the background. Can't think of a better way to wake up from a nap. I look at the time and spring straight up in bed, rushing to smooth down my crazy hair.

I plan on playing her international collection tonight while being on partial mute. That'll help my soundproof issues, preventing anyone from listening in.

Though I don't speak a word of Farsi, Sahrit's ancestors' native language, I find her song called Nowruz mysteriously beautiful. It makes me think of her great-grandparents. As Persian diplomats, they were forced to leave Iran along with the Shah. They went from Iran to Egypt, then to Morocco and for a while, they lived in the Caribbean islands. They finally established themselves in central Mexico in the late 1970's, where they were offered permanent asylum. Sahrit likes to incorporate the rhythms and the flavors of all these countries to her work.

In less than a minute into the meeting, we get to witness Stefan complimenting Sahrit on her music. He asks if she'd consider selling the complete collection, all five albums, to help fund our project. Niiice… he returned with positive input instead of bullying. What a difference a little break makes, combined with a talk with his less impulsive older brother.

"Groovy Idea! Love it!" Sahrit is all smiles.

"Dahvid, could your music production team help put that together?" I add.

Before he can respond, Tomas does, "I'll help you do it, then we can promote it on Liberty World. How does that sound, Jess?"

"Harmonious! How about we have an option to upgrade to retro-vinyl with a funky cover designed by *Mademoiselle Rossé*?" I suggest.

Dahvid waits patiently while we collaborate, until he finds an opening to explain more about our TAP NAP last night. We were allotted one hundred and eighty minutes in the simulation while only ninety seconds of regular time passed. It really works out for the best that we practice this afternoon instead of this morning. Streets should be sparsely populated because most kids will be waking up in time for dinner and going back to sleep, till tomorrow.

He continues, "Soon we will be breaking up into three in-person groups. Jazz has offered to host Jess and Tomas in Scarsdale. She gave me a virtual tour— there's ample space."

Josef and Stefan clear their throats at the same time. I get their not-so-subtle hint and act on it. "What about our junior cadets? There's plenty of room for them, too!"

Dahvid seems a bit on edge. Will he?… Yesss! The first nervous sip of the afternoon! I'm starting to figure him out. I tilt my head forward and my mane covers my amusement.

"We need you to work separately in order to practice using the long-distance audio feature. It would prove to be only half as effective if we are all in close proximity," Dahvid clarifies.

"We could test it by spreading out, couldn't we?" Jazz asks, twirling her swirly, cinnamon tendrils, hoping he'll give in to her irresistible charms— again.

Tomas jumps in, "It'll take the whole six miles between us to keep Stefan focused. He gets way too distracted and shows off when you're around, Jazz. Or haven't you noticed?" Jazz tries very hard not to giggle while Stefan blushes and squirms. He continues, "May I suggest working on being less transparent, it makes one vulnerable. For future missions that could be very dangerous."

"Couldn't have said it better myself, thanks Tomas," Josef states.

Interesting… Tomas is much more insightful than I realized.

Dahvid proceeds, "Each team will go to an open area for the outdoor phase. It needs to be at least twenty minutes away from home base." Dahvid uses his fingers to count the criteria needed for this spot. "One— earth, two— ground cover, three— shrubs or trees, four— mineral formations and five— a body of water. Even under normal circumstances, the area needs to be out of the public eye."

"You know what location I'm going to suggest, don't you?" I ask Jazz.

"Possibly… but you go ahead," she replies humbly.

"All right then… I propose Waterfall Kingdom!"

Tomas, who takes pride in knowing everything about Scarsdale and surrounding areas, reacts, "Whaaat? An amusement park? Where is it? Never heard of it!" He's getting agitated. "I hate those kinds of places, hate the rides, the sound of metal rubbing and clanking. People eating while they're walking. All the smells. Screaming everywhere. No way!"

He couldn't know about this spot, Jazz and I made up the name, years ago. "Tomas, hate to say, but there's a special place in our area you don't know about," I share, with too much of a snarky tone.

Everyone is silent.

Wait— what just happened? I just made an insensitive remark with a sarcastic tone and nothing… no Bleep? No twinge? No nothing? Grrr… I forgot. What's it gonna take to realize that our implants have been deactivated— forever? Am I doomed to being rude and insensitive the rest of my life?

A lavender sphere glides in. "Enjoy the first of your daily breathing reminders. Be patient. New territory. May this conjure all things emerald. Love, The Domestic Goddess." The message departs leaving a healing puff of Mom's new mix. Ahh… how perfectly perfect, now I can apologize. "Tomas, I'm sorry… not having implants is going to take time getting used to."

"I lost my cool too, we're all newbies," he responds.

I smile, nod and explain, "Waterfall Kingdom is an overgrown area near the tracks, behind the station. I assure you it's definitely not an amusement park. Jazz and I played there way before we were superhumans.

Jazz takes over, "When we were about five, we started pretending it was an enchanted garden, filled with gigantic trees, castles, tall towers, secret chambers, even a dragon or two."

"Dragons too? Love it!" Sahrit exclaims, taking in every word.

Tomas goes back to being over reactive, nasty tone and all. "Give me a break and a half—that's so lame. They weren't dragons. They could only have been one of four species of lizards found in New York State. If you're expecting to see fairies, I'm here to tell you they're lightening bugs. You really think we're going to find enchanted creatures going through TAP? You're not kids anymore. Don't be ridiculous!"

Ouch! He's awfully mean without implants. Wonder what his volcanic color is? Hope he remembers to visualize it asap. Dahvid sips, nervously, eyes wide open, saying nothing.

"Tomas, it's fun to be childlike sometimes. Who knows, you might discover something new about yourself to add to your life's story? No one can force you into writing an entry you don't want unless, of course, you want to. Shall we give it a try?" Jazz shares with a caring tone.

While Tomas is pondering, I realize that in the book about my life, Jazz will always be depicted as the fairest fairy of them all!

Dahvid decides to share, "Tomas, have you ever thought of how much inventors, writers, artists, and talented musicians like yourself depend on imagination and fantasy? How else could we channel what we carry inside? Imagination and creativity manifest differently for everyone. You used yours to bring us together and you will also be instrumental in taking down The World Chancellor."

"Hmmm… Well… If you put it that way…"

I can't help myself and remark, "Does that mean you accept, Tomas?"

"*Touché.*" He forces that crooked little smile.

Josef jumps in, "I don't know about you but I want to see where Ms. Stafford initiated her career as a dragon slayer."

"It's a historical landmark!" Stefan follows, waving his invisible sword, making swishing sounds.

My friends see me that brave? Enough to slay dragons in the forest?

"Question: what if the capabilities we lost, were supposed to be temporary?" Sahrit asks.

"That is a very interesting observation. What I can say is that what you will gain by learning to live within TAP will far outweigh the loss of the nano implants. Today's experience promises to be unforgettable. Trust me, you will be transformed forever," Dahvid explains.

"It's exciting to enter a different dimension of understanding. So on that note, I'd like to recommend Dahvid for an additional post," Sahrit shares.

"Really— what is it?" I respond.

"Trust Development Coach."

"Now that's really inspired!" Tomas exclaims and then proceeds to explain how Dahvid earned his trust and benefitted from his friendship and support. They've worked through stuff— really bad stuff— especially lately. He concludes by saying that his way of listening breaks down barriers. "He inspires me to do more… to be more… I'm on board with whatever happens at Waterfall Kingdom."

That's amazing! I need to learn from both Dahvid and Tomas. It takes bravery to show vulnerability. Wait— did I just say that? Applause and cheering bring me back just in time to see Dahvid, he's glowing. Bet he's happier for his friend than having a new title.

"I'm humbled, *mes amis, merci*. We must sign off now to stay on schedule. We are going to need lots of energy for the rest of the day. Please, make sure to eat well and drink plenty of fluids— that goes for… everyone," Dahvid shares with a playful grin. "Let's reconvene in exactly forty-five."

Jazz invites Tomas and I to reconnect off Tower.

"I'm so proud of how you opened up. This calls for a celebration!" she proclaims.

"Can we do it at your house?" he replies.

"But of course! You haven't been inside since it got furnished. Right?"

"Did you have something to do with the front door?" he asks.

"Depends…" Jazz gives him a half grin.

"I rather like it, it's original."

"In that case… I had lots to do with getting the image of my favorite amethyst geode enlarged and transferred onto both sides of our door. Fabulous, isn't it?"

"It really is and so are you," I remark, waving my magic wand. "All right, time to go. See you in forty-five for our next adventure."

Something feels different… I feel… lighter, somehow. Hope it's not because I'm still dizzy. I get out of bed slowly, put my slippers on and go feed my inner child— again.

Dad's office door is open, so he hears my footsteps coming down the stairs. "How're you doing, Princessa?"

"So far… so good… I think."

Mom takes that as a cue and stops what she's doing. She approaches me cautiously and clears strands of hair from my face. She looks me over, up, down and around, making sure I'm all in one piece. I'm guided over to sit on the banquette and she gets back to the food. Even if I can't see her face, I can tell she's crying.

"Mom? Are you okay?"

She nods and sniffs. "Happy tears."

"Thanks for those new sensory reminders… perfectly timed and highly effective." I share, sounding like an advertisement.

"At the Stafford Inn we aim to please. Give me a couple of minutes and lunch will be ready."

From this point on, for the rest of the day, I intend to practice being in the moment. I enjoy watching Mom move about gracefully in Command Central. She opens the fridge and pulls out a multitude of clear glass containers with color coded tops which happen to match their contents. Has she always had them? She lays out shaved vegetables, greens, herbs and fruits, either from our garden or from the Farmer's Market at Hartsdale Station. I can't wait to eat some glossy avocado slivers, crunchy sugar snap peas, cucumbers with juicy steak tomato slices, crisp red and orange pepper strips, and carrot sticks.

Every single colorful element is assembled strategically on a thick slice of her irresistible, homemade multigrain bread which is always toasted to perfection. There's another slice, coated thick with homemade honey mustard ready to receive a steamy turkey burger patty.

"Thank you, Mommy, this is a true labor of love," I say as the incredible, edible tower appears before me. The Stafford Inn Stack is our family's all-time favorite. It takes hours, not a couple of minutes to put together.

Before I dive in, I'm compelled to say, "Hope Jake keeps sleeping."

"I've made plenty for all of us," she remarks with a giggle, as she arranges sliced fruits on the oval hand-painted platter she made at the Rosses art studio.

I swallow my first bite and say, "You know why sleep is the best medicine for Bear?"

Mom plays along, "Umm… I give up… why?"

"Because it's the only thing that keeps him out of the fridge and out of trouble with the law."

Dad comes out of his office, chuckling, rare for him. He's much more serious than Mom. "Glad my clever girl is feeling better," he says, sitting next to me. "After you left this morning, we went upstairs and had the dubious honor of seeing the new addition to Jake's gallery. Care to tell us what happened?"

"Umm… not my place… " I reply, munching on freshly salted, lemony carrots sticks.

Mom changes the subject, "I made *aguas frescas.* We have watermelon hibiscus or lemon lime mint…"

"Tough one. I'm in an adventurous mood, so I'll have both!" Dad seconds the motion.

Mom comes back with the pitchers, "Jesse Girl, please slow down. You're not chewing— you're inhaling. What's the rush?" If she only knew about TAP, she'd have to eat her words. I cough, almost choke, laughing at my own clever line.

"See what I mean?" she says as she pours the *aguas frescas* into two bubbled glasses with cobalt rims. She's made her special ice cubes. Some have little herbs, and others have edible flowers inside. I love hearing them crack and shift.

"Any way to package and sell these lovely frozen cubettes?" I ask, thinking of ways to increase her sales.

She giggles, "Nice idea, but even in winter, I don't think they'd travel well."

I continue admiring the decorations on the drinks. One glass has a small red flower, piercing through the center of lime and lemon slices. The other has a salted watermelon cube with mint sprigs, artistically attached.

"As Jazz would say, this is gorgeously

delicious! Mom, you— are— so— talented. I really mean it!" Wonder if I've ever taken the time to compliment her before.

"Thank you, Sweetie, I'm so touched," Mom says as Dad lovingly reaches for her hand.

Guess I haven't. Bleep! Shame on me.

"Jazz, Tomas and I… need to process our experience from this morning. We've been invited across the street after lunch. Is that okay?" Did I just lie or was that a creative interpretation of the truth? I award myself… half a Chime.

Dad replies, "It makes perfect sense to share your impressions with someone who's gone through the same experience."

To which Mom adds, "Just please do us all a favor, check in from time to time. Let us know what you're up to."

"We may go for a walk later. We should be back in a couple of hours…"

"Jeeesss?"

"Yes ma'am!" I salute a la Tallon-Saldane.

Now outside, I study Jazz's house, from our front steps. It looks so different now, hard to believe it used to be an old, rundown house, like ours, built over a century ago. Story goes both were owned by one family and went up for sale at the same time. Originally, my parents wanted to buy that house because it's on a larger lot and on a hill. Mom had her heart set on having a huge garden. After our talk, I can understand why. Dad used to joke about our acoustically challenged, creaky shoe box of a house. "It would be more fruitful to put money into the ground, water it and wait for a money tree to grow, than to pay for all the repairs."

After several years of research and planning, the Rosses opted to knock the whole rickety-rackety thing down and start over. The building was demolished, the materials were recycled by the coolest company ever. They sorted the debris and mixed it with different composites, then processed by a Mega Klôner. All the sections were customized and manufactured with the necessary plumbing and electrical components. The assembly of the giant puzzle was such an anticipated event that friends and neighbors came with lawn chairs to watch. It was even featured on the news. Jazz and her young assistant decided to enhance their guests' experience by serving— what else, Himalayan salted popcorn and pink lemonade.

As I walk up to the amethyst front door, I remember when the Rosses placed large pieces of randomly cut slate to cover these steps. At the time, ours were puny, uneven crumbling, concrete, prehistoric monoliths. Dad kept saying he'd get to them when he finished all the other repairs— he never did.

One weekend, we went away to celebrate Mom's birthday. Mr. Ross, along with little Sy's expertise, snuck over and installed their leftover multicolor pieces on our steps. Mom didn't see their gift till the day after we got back. Seems like she cried for days.

My index finger is poised to initiate their digital lock system when Sy opens the door.

"*Bonjour Mam'selle*," he bows, "do you have a reservation?"

"*Oui, Monsieur,*" I reply, bowing back at him.

The handsome concierge with deep, blue, Maui-ocean eyes escorts me to the stairway. He then dashes off, as if ice skating on the wood floor, in his socked feet.

My mind slows down, and my body relaxes whenever I'm here. Is it because it's so open and uncomplicated or is it because it always smells fresh? Maybe it's that majestic view straight ahead. The whole back of this house is glass and overlooks an overgrown, wooded area. Here, in the den, there's a choice of how to enjoy the panorama. The most dramatic is the *Al Fresco* option, where the glass panels fold on themselves and hide within wall pockets on either side. The other version allows for the widows to open, while the wall-to-wall panels remain closed. To make it even cooler, the panels themselves become an enormous Glåsse or several different ones. I stare in amazement.

"Jess… feeling okay, Babe?" Jazz's mom calls out. She sees me from her office.

"Oh, hi Aunt Dani… yes… thanks… I was just recharging my battery. Glad to see *Monsieur Sy* is intact."

"Amazing, isn't it? Considering what he's been through, our Little Man is quite adaptable and resilient. Can I get you anything before you go upstairs for your appointment?"

I shake my head, smile and put my hands on my flat, but very full tummy. "I just finished a huge meal— enough for six."

"So I hear… sounds like you woke up with quite an appetite," she chuckles.

"Yup! We're way overdue for a conversation."

"You bet! Jess— remember that this home and the view are as much yours as they are ours," she replies warmly. I love her so much.

My effort to stay in the moment continues as I walk up the stairs slowly. I reach the top and recall the story about this… Mr. Ross was on a photoshoot expedition when he came across an abandoned foundry. He spotted piles and piles of old, rusted metal sheets. He spent hours choosing the best ones and propping them against the fence. He captured tons of cool images and shared them with Jazz. She determined that they just couldn't live without any of them. As a surprise, her dad had two of the sheets cut down and sealed, making sure the rust and the many layers of old paint were left intact. The spectacular panels are what cover both sides of her bedroom door.

I use our special, secret knock. The door slides open and hides into a pocket in the wall. The pocket has a built-in nightlight that turns on automatically when it starts getting dark. To me, it means— all roads lead to Jazz.

"*Bonjour*, Fearless Leader," Jazz calls out, siting at her desk. "Tomas says he's running a few minutes late."

"Can't wait to hear his comments about your house. Do you think he sees colors differently than we do? He definitely sees the world differently. Wouldn't you love to know what his hue.r.u quotient is?"

"We all see colors differently. I don't see him divulging any of that intentionally."

"May I look around till he gets here?" I ask, placing my arms behind my back like a detective.

"Sure, I have to concentrate," she responds. We both know that means— be quiet.

Pretending never to have been in Jazz's room before, I'm taking it all in, starting with the pink ceiling. The chandelier looks like a cluster of faceted rhinestones. As the intensity of the light spreads out, the paint becomes paler and paler as it goes down the walls, until it blends with the off-white trim. The floor has irregular-sized natural wood planks with an ergonomic texture. It feels great when we're barefoot. It's stained in what Jazz describes as definitely not gray and definitely not brown, but a wondrous color known as taupe. Her closet is in a league of its own. They used theatrical lighting for tonal accuracy, which as she explains, gives the contents of her mini boutique— pizzazz! The best part, as far as I'm concerned, is when she outgrows clothes or loses interest in something. I'm first in line for her top shelf hand-me-downs, including her bedding. That happened once her famous cappuccino sectional/sofa bed arrived. Even though it was below freezing, she insisted on waiting outside to watch the delivery truck making its last turn onto our street.

"Why do we have to do this? It's freezing!" I asked rubbing my cold hands and stomping my boots, trying to wake my numb feet.

"So I'll know they were careful driving all the way over here!" Jazz replies. She was as excited, as I was jealous. Had I brought my device outside, it would have been an intense orangey-red, a perfect segue way to what happened next.

"Did I tell you the pieces are coming from Italy?" she asked for the umpteenth time, "don't you just love everything Italian?"

What did I know or care about Italian anything? To hide my disdain, I went into default which was and still is— sarcasm.

"Oh, I dooo! In fact, I absolutely love ricotta-filled cannelloni a la marinara. Don't you?"

Jazz said nothing, but those folded arms over the chest move and the stomping of both feet said it all. My saucy comment had made her very mad. Thankfully, we survived the frigid episode. Most importantly, her room was featured in an article about creating wonderful multi-purpose rooms for kids.

Working my way to the sectional, I get a closer look of the sunset picture that matches Zivah Zahav's book cover. How can I find out more without raising suspicions? "Hey! Why are you inspecting my picture so closely? Looking for a buried treasure in the sand?" she asks.

"One never knows, *Mademoiselle…*" I reply, with a playful French accent.

"It's that kind of picture, isn't it? I keep discovering things."

"Really? Like what?"

"Tomas! You made it earlier than I thought!" Jazz exclaims.

Grrr… what poor timing, he ruined my chance to get answers to my burning questions.

"I managed my time differently, so I'd be able to look inside before our meeting." Turning away to look at the hallway, he adds, "The stairs are radical. Each tread is a different wood species. You know that, right?"

She giggles, "Yes, I do know that, and I'm not surprised you picked up on it."

Wanting to be part of the conversation, I add, "Did you know that the bannister was made from a tree that fell during a storm? They installed it not that long ago."

Tomas replies unfazed with that tone of his, "Did you know that I saw the moment lightning struck a tree on our way back from the airport, not that long ago? Where did the idea of these stairs come from?"

"Gorgeous, right? My parents saw it in a design book they got as a gift."

"Do they still have the book?" I continue my detective work, wondering if it's Zivah's.

"Since when are you so interested in interior design, Ms. Stafford?" Jazz asks, placing her hands on her hips.

"You lead by example." I mimic her pose.

"Tomas, you don't plan on holding onto the door frame all afternoon, do you?"

"My sister has very strict rules about anyone, well— really me, coming into her room without asking. Figured I'd wait here."

"Come in!" She waves him inside with a smile.

"Are we going to sit on the floor, Japanese style, so we don't mess up all those fancy pillows on the sofa?" he wonders.

"Your sister has trained you well," I joke. He rolls his eyes.

"Check this out!" Jazz says, tapping on her device. Out from underneath the sectional slide out a collapsed table and three chairs. The fourth is by her desk.

"Jazz is into Italian-everything, you know," I say, with an extra dose of snobbiness.

"*Bellissimo!*" he responds, with perfect Italian pronunciation. As the rest of the gang joins us, Tomas greets them, "*Buon giorno a tutti!*"

Dahvid announces we need to start asap. Code is ready to produce the next set of drops in our Micro Klôners. He reviews how to prepare our surroundings, since we're doing this in groups. Extra space is necessary for when the drops are absorbed by our bodies.

"What does that mean, exactly?" Tomas is sounding nervous.

Dahvid avoids answering directly. "Jazz, Jess, Tomas— your kits will each have three separate amber-colored vials. The timer will prompt you and pause after each application. The drops must be applied in a particular order, beginning with the oculars. Start with the right eye, five drops for each eye for a total of ten. Next apply one drop for each audio and lastly, one for the olfactos. During and after the series is dispensed, you must lay still until I say otherwise, not a moment sooner. You may experience anything from tickling to itching to slight burning, or you may just go into a dream-like state. These symptoms will be relatively short lived, so breathe your way through them."

He pauses for a turquoise sip. "Josef and Stefan, you will receive an additional set of oral drops, specifically designed for the military. Do those drops last. Follow my instructions to initiate the process, after that we will be on mute to avoid distractions. Seems we had a technical glitch, before."

No wonder I heard him speaking to Josef.

"Do we alternate the ocular drops or do five and five?" Tomas asks, sounding even more agitated.

"They have to be alternated. Thank you for catching that omission," Dahvid responds.

"There's so much to this, can we help each other?" Jazz wonders.

How considerate. She knows how to help Tomas without embarrassment. I always learn so much from her, if I only applied it.

"Chimes…" I whisper under my breath, "I sure miss hearing from you."

"Helping one another is what life is all about. That's why I'm at Sahrit's recording studio," Dahvid remarks.

"Is her studio somewhere… on planet Earth?" Tomas quips, alluding to Maarlee's tag line.

Sahrit giggles and gives him a thumbs up.

I jump in, "Dahvid, you just said you'd be helping Sahrit and not the other way around. Sounds like you haven't fully disclosed some things. Have you already had the drops applied?" Uh, oh… that ugly, accusatory debate tone of mine has shown its ugly head. Jazz touches my hand to stop me from going any further, but it's too late. If the implants were still working, I'd get a very loud Bleep!

Dahvid blinks quickly. He straightens up in his seat, takes a couple of gulps and responds, "As a matter of fact, Ms. Stafford, yes, I already have the drops in me…"

Ouch! We're back on a last name basis— I deserve it.

"…as do Jordan and Leonardo. It was the only way we could test, refine, perfect, and feel comfortable sharing this tech. Our top priority is to protect everyone, including you and your group."

Shame on me for feeling tricked or lied to by Dahvid, of all people!

Jazz points at her device which says:

> Humility isn't thinking less of yourself,
> it's about thinking of yourself, less.
> ~ CS Lewis.

I feel embarrassed and amused at the same time. I now have human thought interrupters.

"Dahvid, does your body feel differently after taking the drops?" Stefan wonders. "How were you able to test the drops if you still had the implants?" Josef cuts in. "Do you experience life differently than before?" Tomas adds.

"Thank you for your excellent questions. First and foremost, there's something important you need to know about the drops. Once they are applied, do not— I repeat, do not, under any circumstances, rub your eyes, nose or ears. And— even if you are tempted, do not drink or eat anything afterwards, for at least thirty minutes," Dahvid instructs.

"If you tell me not to do something, I'm going to feel compelled to do it— that's just me," I blurt out. Everyone, except for Dahvid, laughs because they know it's true.

"Are there ways to predetermine who'll feel what?" Tomas asks.

"We have not focused our research on that, but it's definitely an interesting point for future consideration."

In a preemptive move, Tomas asks Jazz if he can borrow some gloves, they'd help remind him not to touch or scratch.

"Sure! Will any color work?"

"I'd prefer peacock blue as a first choice or dark blue second."

Dahvid continues, "As for experiencing life differently— absolutely! Taking this on is a huge responsibility, but also a privilege that provides a thrill that defies explanation."

"That should motivate us to work through any discomfort," I remark with Tomas in mind.

Was I the only one who noticed how skillfully Dahvid skipped over the second question? I want to know how he, Jordan, Leonardo, and who-knows-who-else experimented with the drops while they still had implants. How can I approach this nicely? Should I start by asking what's in that beautiful, iridescent turquoise thermos of his? No— better not, I've upset him enough in a very short time.

Dahvid announces we have three minutes to prepare. Jazz jumps into action and hands us our freshly minted kits. Each amber vial has a dark brown top with a dropper attached. The tiny sepia label has dark brown schematics.

"Aren't these just divinely, irresistibly cute?" Jazz comments.

"Fabulous, just fabulous, dahling," I reply, with my best British accent. "Have you thought of ways to use them afterwards— earrings perhaps?"

"Stupendous idea, indeed," she responds.

"Stop! Stop right this minute!" Tomas exclaims.

"Why… what's wrong?" Jazz is startled by his tone.

"Dahvid was quite clear, we have to save the vials, no arts and crafts stuff!" Tomas reminds us with that tone of his.

"We're just being playful, you took us literally. Don't worry, I'm well prepared. We're keeping ours safe in this special little box. See?" She shows us a black cardboard box with an attached top. The interior is padded with scrunched up brown paper.

Jazz is masterful at defusing Tomas from

anxiety producing scenarios. I'm starting to notice that his responses aren't necessarily proportionate to the situation. Wait— that sounds just like… Am I finding parallels between Tomas and… is that why I find him so annoying? He reminds me of me? No— no way, I can't go there— not now!

I hyper focus on Ms. Ross, who has transitioned seamlessly into her role as space planner. She points at one of the end tables as being mine so I can reach for the vial with my right hand, when we sit on the sectional. How thoughtful. Then, the collapsible table glides back underneath. I'm instructed to stack the three chairs against the wall while Tomas repositions the rug in the middle of the room, giving him more space to lie on it comfortably. Jazz hands him a large slice of polished petrified wood to use as his flat surface. Before setting it on the floor, he studies it very carefully and says, "Should you decide to discard this old piece of wood, I'll be more than glad to remove it from the premises for you— at no charge."

"Why would I do that?" Jazz plays along.

"I find it to be inconsistent with the overall decor," Tomas replies, exaggerating his already snobby tone.

"You are much too kind, Sir Tomas, but it so happens that this piece has been in our family for millennia. Besides, it's *tres chic* to combine antiques with modern decor. You know that, right?"

"*Touché,*" he replies, carefully placing the magnificent piece on the rug.

Our hostess distributes soft throws gracefully. Two land on the sectional just so, the other, on the rug along with a couple of pillows. She takes a step back to observe the results. "*Tré bien!*" Our prima ballerina's moves remind me of her dance recital a few weeks ago. After the performance, her parents handed her a bouquet of pink and white roses. She tossed some at her adoring audience.

Jazz brings me back when she says, "Ms. Stafford… the floor is yours."

On cue, I go into leadership mode, "I'll put the drops in you and you in me. Tomas— you'll supervise us. Then we can help you." I hold my breath, waiting for his reaction.

"Drops are really hard for me. So… Jazz… will you help me with that part? Jess, you can supervise," he determines.

Surprisingly, I'm not jealous, not jealous at all, I'm relieved. Tomas and I get on each other's nerves most of the time, so messing this up could lead to disaster.

Dahvid reappears with Sahrit and Jazz announces, "*Maestro*, we're ready for you."

"Excellent!" he replies. The screen shows the same instructions printed on the tiny labels, along with a timer.

We can't see Josef or Stefan, but we can hear them speaking to each other.

"Josef, where are you?" I call out.

"The bunk beds are too confining, so we're on the floor. We don't want to get injured nor do we want to damage any government property."

"It would be impossible to explain what happened," Stefan adds.

Dahvid agrees and continues, "Since we are helping one another, you each need to say— 'done!' with emphasis, as you complete your full round. The voice recognition system will reset the timer for the next person until everyone is finished."

"That's why you needed to capture my voice!"

"Precisely, Ms. Stafford— for those who choose to wear gloves, put them on after all the drops have been dispensed. I will now mute the system so we can begin."

Mission accomplished, no incidents to report. Jazz is relaxing and I'm waiting for something to happen. Until it does, I decide to focus on a ray of afternoon sunlight streaming through a window. The spotlight is featuring Mr. Tomas Kesher. He's lying flat on his back, so still and peaceful, no movement, no twitching. Did Jazz teach him how to go into a deep meditative state? Wish I could learn, but how do I overcome my discomfort of being in total silence? I clear my throat, Tomas groans.

Jazz's sleepy eyes open. She points at me and starts laughing louder and louder. What did I miss? She's snorting and holding her folded legs against her stomach, rolling side to side. Hope she doesn't fall off the sectional and hit her head on the floor.

"Jazz Ross, this is so unlike you! Your behavior is terribly unladylike— I love it! Thank you for the entertainment."

I feel compelled to create a fashion narrative. One, because her *ensemble* is so *je ne sais quoi* and two because I love her laughter.

"Ladies and gentlemen, *Mademoiselle Rossé,* Fashionista to the Stars, is launching her new look this afternoon. Notice the oversized, olive cargo pants paired with an enormous, brown t-shirt full of minute holes and rips. The overly casual pieces complement each other perfectly. *Mademoiselle Rossé* has expertly accessorized with not one, but two different, multi-colored ankle socks with crazy geometric patterns. What can we say about those pink satin Cinderella gloves that go above the elbows other than… *très magnifique!"*

Jazz is crying and laughing, begging for me to stop. She ends up sliding to the floor. I ignore her pleas and keep going, "Behold her exquisite, pink diamond tiara made of the finest plastique. It features the largest pink dangling center stone ever seen, *circa* 2030. Though her twirly, whirly, cinnamon hair is all over the place, note how her crown remains affixed onto her regal head."

"Uh, oh… something's not right… " I say, breaking out of character. Tickling sensations are quickly shifting to itching and burning. I can't put my emerald gloves on fast enough. Jazz keeps laughing because she thinks I'm still performing for her. She starts narrating, describing my flailing arms and legs as an inevitable invasion of giant bugs from another galaxy.

"Stop! I'm having a beyond awful reaction."

Jazz's hysterical laughter ends abruptly. We hear Tomas mumbling as he crawls towards the small chairs. He chooses one, positions it facing the wall, sits on it and continues the animated, conversation.

Kaaa-plunk!

"Oh nooo! This is terrible!" Jazz exclaims in a panic. "Tomas is on the floor!"

"The Italian chair, it's destroyed!" I yell out, stunning Tomas out of his hallucination.

"What happened? Where am I? Why am I on the floor?"

"Tomas, it's me, Jazz. Stop— don't get up, don't even move, stay on the floor. Okay?"

"Okay! But what happened? I need to know!" he responds anxiously with arms up in the air.

She turns to me and whispers, "Good thing he was barely off the ground. This must be one of the other TAP side effects. We've entered Crazyville!"

"But can you get another chair?" I ask. My unintentional joke upsets Tomas even more.

"Jess, this isn't funny. Chairs come and go but Tomas Kesher is unique, he's irreplaceable!" she exclaims.

How could I be so thoughtless? I feel horrible and remorseful for being so unconcerned.

"Bleeeep!" I blurt out, loudly. Jazz gives me a dirty look, wondering why I'm making such a ridiculous sound at a time like this.

Dahvid is back on the screen. "You may sit up now. I am eager to hear how everyone is doing. Any impressions or experiences to share?"

Tomas, still holding his arms up, uses his socked heels to rotate and face Dahvid. "I have no idea what just happened here, other than I've destroyed a fine piece of imported Italian furniture. I won't move so Jazz can collect all the residue. There may be a way to produce a new chair in her Klôner."

Jazz touches her heart, pouts and says, "that's so very thoughtful of you. Please, don't worry, it's just a silly chair."

"Tomas, does anything hurt?" Dahvid sounds concerned.

"No, I don't think so. Well… to be honest… yes, my pride. What a klutz, I can't even sit on a chair without breaking it," he responds, looking at his gloves, pants and socks covered in off-white powder, previously known as a chair.

Dahvid explains that what happened was a result of the high speed at which we were traveling. After reassuring Tomas that the incident has nothing to do with lacking grace, he directs himself towards Josef and Stefan. They are very serious and annoyingly quiet. "Gentlemen, anything to report?" Being now visible, all they do is shake their heads. How could they have zero questions to ask? Why aren't they exhibiting any signs of discomfort or distress? Their lack of desire or ability to express their emotions drives me up the wall and out the window!

Jazz turns to me, we mimic their serious faces and their head shaking. Sahrit can't contain her giggles.

"As wonderful as it is to see you ladies having so much fun, we need to move on. Please try to control yourselves," Dahvid instructs, flashing his gorgeous smile.

Tomas speaks up, "It is my observation that uncontrollable laugh attacks, when entering TAP may have a direct correlation to high levels of estrogen found in adolescent girls."

These adolescent girls find that really funny so we burst out laughing, again.

"Thank you for that observation," Dahvid replies, blushing. "Time for us to go outdoors. The temperature in your area will be dropping steadily, so dress accordingly. No need to use your devices. We have already synced the new internals, it will appear as if we are face-to-face with each other."

"Oh my stars, how cool!" Sahrit exclaims.

Tomas is very excited, but nevertheless, remembers to return the powdery gloves back to Jazz. She offers them as a souvenir of his high-speed adventure. As we admire the stairway again, Dahvid announces he wants to share more about himself, during our walk.

"It's about time— considering you know pretty much everything about us," I share, hoping I've used the right tone. Must have, Jazz didn't Bleep! me.

Jazz opens the front door. How I love cold crisp air on my face. It helps me focus. She and I interlock arms and put our hands back in our pockets, just like we've done since childhood. Tomas walks a couple of paces behind us. Jazz turns to face him, walking backwards, she asks, "Ready to fully experience Waterfall Kingdom?"

"Ready!" he exclaims, catching up with us.

Dahvid follows, "Ready to hear my story?"

"Don't think we can wait a nanosecond longer," Jazz replies with her wonderful giggle.

HOURS
ACT IX

🌐 Monday, March 4, 2041, 5:03 PM

"You are about to experience something which happened to me in the past." Dahvid begins to narrate, his image disappears and a scene unfolds before us...

"I find myself at a large office with *El Señor Inspector*. He is wearing a fake looking, overly decorated, military uniform. We sit at a large table. He asks that I state my name, for the record."

"Dahvid Toledano."

"What an unusual name," the man comments.

"It was designed by my ancestors in Spain and given to me by my grandfather."

The inspector looks puzzled, he asks that I explain further.

"It was designed by my ancestors, centuries ago, to be given to me at birth. My name was carefully arranged, tying every letter to whom I'd be destined to become."

The inspector is puzzled but decides to move on. He directs his words to the assistant sitting next to him, "Let it be noted that the table before us will be used to display the items in question." Without looking up, the assistant stands and using both of her dark coat's sleeves, wipes off my side of the surface. She finishes the highly dusty process and nods, indicating I can begin.

There is a tattered carpet bag next to me from which I pull some objects. First, a heavily carved box. I open it and tilt it to show the aged lining inside. I place it on the table and produce a folded scarf with blue and white designs, outlined in gold. Next, comes a glossy, sapphire blue ribbon, rolled onto an old, wooden spool.

"I believe something is missing, is it not?" the inspector remarks, firmly.

I nod, wipe the table again with my own sleeves, collecting more dust. The last item is placed on the table. The inspector uses a black lacquer pointer to refer to the four items.

"For the record, how did you acquire these?"

"Two years ago, shortly before my thirteenth birthday, my grandfather told me he had a special gift for me. He instructed me to close my eyes, extend both arms straight out, palms up, ring fingers and pinkies touching. He placed an object, so heavy that it made my hands drop down from the weight. Even if I wanted to look, I kept my eyes closed because I always wait for his instructions."

"Commendable behavior," *El Señor Inspector* interrupts. He proceeds to dictate that going forward, the document will refer to the last object as Exhibit A, the box as B, the scarf as C, and ribbon as D.

"For the record, describe Exhibit A."

"It is a very old, leather bound book, the third page is thicker than the rest," I reply.

"Is anything on the third page?" he asks.

"Yes, it is an entry written with quill and ink."

"How do you know about quill and ink?"

"My grandfather has always shown great reverence for history. I have seen him create mysterious undulating letters like these, on parchment, like a scribe, in times gone by."

The inspector moves along. "Do you know what language the entry is in?"

"No, sir, but when my grandfather reads, somehow, I am able to understand."

The inspector, looking intrigued, strokes his mustache and beard. "Open the book and read the entry, young man."

I take a deep breath and whisper three times:

"*Jaime De Los Reyes De Córdoba Toledano.*"

"What did you just say?" the inspector seems upset.

"*Perdón… estoy muy nervioso.*"

The assistant encourages me not to be afraid and to read.

"We are eternally grateful to the Almighty for allowing us to witness this long-awaited event. We pray that this child is loving and obedient, a faithful student and follower of 'The Truth.' May he be a respectable member of society, able to fulfill his intended purpose in life. As a family, may we continue to alleviate the difficulties and challenges, plaguing humanity since the beginning of time. In honor of our ancestors, we name you…"

Dahvid stops in mid-sentence, takes a deep breath and exhales, loudly. He then continues, "My heart was beating so fast, realizing I was about to divulge the sacred version of my name that… I woke up!"

"C'mon… seriously? This was just a dream?" I say with what I hope is an appropriately annoyed tone, "What's the point of this?"

Jazz tugs really hard on my right sleeve, which must equal a fully loaded Bleep!

He replies cryptically, "Soon you will learn, as I did, that there is no such thing as just a dream."

Tomas interjects, "Dahvid, you've never told me about this dream. There's so much to it."

"My grandfather has taught me many things, including the power of patience, good timing, and great storytelling." We hear the smile in his voice, "We have reached our destination, so it is time to move on to the next phase."

"Ohhh nooo you don't! You can't just leave us hanging like this! You have to finish the story. What's a little extra time among friends if were already TAP dancing?" Jazz exclaims.

"Such a clever, clever girl," Stefan remarks, sarcastically.

I jump in, "As you now know, some of us are famous for our impatience and some for our sarcasm— or both. Does your grandfather happen to offer tutoring?" I ask with a chuckle.

Dahvid chuckles back and replies, "Lito, as I call him, is an extremely busy man."

"Explain why he's called Lito," Sahrit remarks.

"Lito is short for *abuelito,* an endearing term used for grandfather, in our family. Every moment with him is a life lesson. For example, one of them inspired me to design the tech we are using right now. It captures and replays memories and dreams in vivid detail. In case you were wondering what I said in the dream, it was Lito's full name, which was also constructed to be a source of comfort and reassurance. Should anyone in our immediate family feel afraid, whether awake or asleep, we are permitted to pronounce it, but no more than three times in a row. It is guaranteed to banish negative or uncomfortable feelings."

"Wish I had a grandfather with a name like that. Wish I had grandfather, period…" Tomas shares longingly.

Dahvid continues, "As you heard, that dream happened two years ago, and two nights after that, we were invited to my grandparents' NYC apartment. That is where we celebrated my unforgettably surprising thirteenth birthday."

A new scene appears. We see Dahvid knocking on a door, which opens by itself. He smiles and plays along, because he hears young children giggling behind it.

Dahvid begins the narration, "My parents, younger brother, sister and I walk into the living room and see Lito and Lita standing by an enormous box. Now, my not-so-invisible, costume-wearing twin cousins rush over to join them.

"*¡Felíz cumpleaños, Dahvid!*" they exclaim.

I could not wait to see what was inside. But as I had told *El Señor Inspector* in the dream, I always wait for instructions.

"Open it, dear boy," Lito instructs, "how else can you embark on the adventure that will launch the rest of your life's journey?"

Sitting on the sofa, across from everyone, I inspect the oversized box.

"*Chicos... recuerden, el papel es un arte.* Paper is an art form, and much like a painting on a canvas, we must savor every inch. Don Jaime, this is the most beautiful paper I have ever seen, *está precioso!*" my mami exclaims.

Lito smiles ear to ear, "*Que bueno que te gusta, Anita.* Part of this gift is for you, too. Had you not agreed to marry my son, we wouldn't be here, celebrating Dahvid's birth."

Everyone is staring, waiting anxiously as I pop the flaps open. Inside are layers upon layers of tissue paper. Lito instructs me to remove them, carefully, one by one. The last sheet of tissue is out of the box. At the bottom is a miniature bird's nest, filled with small polished blue stones. I thank Lito for the lovely gift. He smiles, outstretching his arms, offering to hold it. There is still more inside. I reach in and feel a rectangular shape, covered in silky fabric, just like in the dream.

"*Dahvid, cariño,*" Lita speaks softly, "before you proceed, take a look at our rose onyx coffee table. Being patient can be rewarding and creative."

A stack of colored tissue, as tall as my younger sister, charts the order in which it was removed. The very bottom layer of the ethereal sculpture is cloud white, then, palest of blues to noon sky. The top is cloaked by rich purply-blue, a color only a special few get to see at sunset. The very same color as the blue sapphire cluster that lives on Lito's desk.

"This is so beautiful. I was so focused on getting to the gift that I missed the beauty of the tissue itself," I explain.

"Indeed, my dear boy, one must appreciate everything that is happening around us, at the time it is happening. Time itself is a gift. I want you to imagine that each tissue represents a moment in your future. There will be situations when you will be presented with simple decisions or others, more complex that may involve more than one person. Then there will be other scenarios where your choices could affect the whole of humanity. You must remember to be focused, methodical, patient and restrained. These qualities and practices will get you closer to living The Ultimate Truth."

"Lito, when I hear you speak, I see colors, which produce musical notes within me. Right now they are coming together as a beautiful melody. They are dancing around your words."

Tears start to form in my grandfather's eyes. Lita, pats his hand, gets up and sits by me, speaking almost in a whisper, "*Vidito de mi alma*, I want you to also remember that it is the little things that matter most." She takes my head with both hands, tilts it forward, planting six loving kisses, in the usual order.

"Lita, I am tasting the flavors and many layers of your delicate phyllo dough, the one that takes you hours to prepare. Do you have any of those delicious diamond shaped pistachio baklavas? It is that time of year…"

She nods, smiles, gets up, stands behind Lito, squeezes his shoulders and walks into the kitchen with her head down.

"Why is she so sad, Lito? I love her baklavas… We all do!"

"It is difficult to explain, but sometimes overflowing joy can make us feel sad." He reaches for an embroidered handkerchief, wiping away his tears. Lita returns with a large silver tray, covered with her famous honey kissed delicacies. Lito instructs that before we enjoy the irresistible treats, I must open the last gift— carefully. I remove the blue, white and gold silk covering and offer it to my delighted mother who notices that the pattern is very much like the paper on the box. She folds the scarf in half, like a triangle and wraps it around my sister's neck. Everyone is staring at a pewter box. The elaborate carvings give me the sense that some of the flattened areas were created by sorrows.

"Open it, open it!" exclaims our audience.

Inside the hinged box is an old leather bound book. It is covered in tiny gold velvet flecks that have been sloughing off the inner lining, probably for centuries.

I slide the golden dust gently off the book, making sure every spec remains in its ancient container. The third page, marked with a blue ribbon, is blank. I look up at Lito, with an obvious question in my eyes.

"Return the book to the case and come with me," he says softly. The young members of the audience express their disappointment, having to stay behind. He leads me down the hallway and we enter through a narrow door I had never seen before. Lito pulls the cord on a single bare bulb in the small, windowless room. I wonder, but do not dare ask, why he thinks today is the best day to teach me how photographs were developed in the early 1800's. As he immerses sheets of paper in shallow tubs of odorous fluids, images of Argentina's varied landscape begin to appear, as if by magic.

"This is and will continue to be the most precise method of expressing oneself as a true visionary. It takes great dedication and patience to learn one's craft. It is alchemy at its best! As you become ready for knowledge, it appears on the pages of your life, just as photographs do on wet paper."

"We return to the living room just in time to catch my little cousin, Mia in action. Dressed like Queen Esther, she is grabbing the last few pieces of baklava that had been saved for us."

"Arggg!" Uriel, the pirate, Mia's twin brother, jumps onto the rolled arm of a chair. "You abandon ship, we take treasures hostage!"

"That is a steep ransom. Do you think it is fair, *Coronel Piedra Buena*?" Lito remarks.

"The world is not fair!" the pirate snaps back, shifting from anger to sadness."

Queen Esther returns the pastry treasure trove, placing it carefully, next to the celestial stack, on the coffee table. She reaches for her brother's hand; they walk away.

"Lito, do you really believe that Tía Mariana and Tío Micael survived 'The Event' or is that to make Mia and Urielito feel better?

"I speak from the heart. Hope is the gift that sustains us through hard times, " he sighs.

We sit in silence until he determines it is time to open the leather bound book again. Words materialize before my eyes…

Dahvid De Los Angeles De Córdoba

Toledano, descendant of Spanish mystics
from Córdoba and Toledo.
Receive this bounty of gifts and talents,
for you are The Chosen One.
Embrace the honor with humility
for you have been granted
privilege and responsibility.
You shall right the wrongs of the world.
You cannot do this alone.
Choose wisely.

Dahvid stops abruptly and requests that we never use his grandfather's or his full name— ever. That can only happen in specific circumstances, with their knowledge and consent. Then there's silence.

"What happened? Why did he stop? He knows we're holding on to his every word." I demand from Jazz.

She leans over and, in a whisper, explains, "It must be super intense to relive one's dreams and memories. He's exhausted. In ancient times, prophecy and revelations came to people through dreams or trances. I have experiences like that, just much more diluted, and use terms like premonition or intuition. I had that today."

"What are you talking about— Jazz?"

"That's part of why I was so anxious this morning. I sensed that the four of us had to be together or Jake would be in big trouble."

"How do you know if it's intuition or telepathy?"

"It's hard to explain unless you're living it. Once you're open to 'receiving' and 'sharing' info this way, it happens more and more…"

Weird things are definitely happening in the dawn of this post-implant era. I'm intrigued—how could she have known about Jake? Maybe I have some of that, too. After all, I did refer to myself as The Chosen One.

Dahvid creates a written message, letting us know that the meeting will reconvene shortly. At which time, our audio and visual capabilities will be fully restored. Now it's harder than ever to wait patiently, outside Waterfall Kingdom.

Dahvid reappears seven minutes later. His hands are hiding behind his back. "I hope that was not too lengthy of a story. It had to be told before entering the next phase of training. Now that you can see me, it is time to show you the actual book."

He's wearing lightweight, white gloves, the kind used by people who handle ancient artifacts. He asks Jazz to read the gold embossed title out loud.

"*Mundo De Libertad,*" she says as her knees buckle. Tomas and I catch her and guide her down slowly to the pavement. I'm not letting go of my best friend— she's looking faint.

"Everything okay there in Scarsdale? You are uncharacteristically silent," Dahvid remarks.

Jazz lets go of my hand and reaches into her pouch. Out comes a clear bottle and magenta top, filled with her favorite Pink Ambrosia energy drink. After a few loud gulps, that sweet smile we all love reappears.

"Based on your reaction, I am guessing there must be quite a story to complement mine. Jess, how did you come up with the name for your communication platform, Liberty World? Our research team could not find anything."

I take a deep breath and hold onto Jazz's hand again. "Dahvid… the time has come to tell the truth. It was Jazz— it's been her from the very beginning. I may have had the general idea about creating a group, but she came up with the name. After the last debate, my membership skyrocketed within the first hour. It was overwhelming— I panicked. Jazz agreed to take over— just like that!" I say, snapping my fingers. "She came up with the mission statement, the questions, the tech— all of it!"

"Let me get this straight— Jazz came up with the same name in English as the book's title without realizing it? *Fascinante…*" Tomas comments, showing off his Spanish while stroking his non-existent beard, mimicking *El Señor Inspector.*

"The name came to me during meditation. I was in another dimension. It just felt right," Jazz explains, with eyes sparkling.

Josef skips right over this huge revelation and asks, "What's the connection between your ancestors' book and TAP?"

"Everything I will ever need to know and everything I will need to share with you is right here. This ancient text was designed for us to attain our joint goal— saving the world. We are about to witness some of its sacred contents interpreted, here in the open. The experience was designed by some of our talented team members," Dahvid shares with noticeable excitement.

Mademoiselle Rossé is completely taken in. Sahrit, our *chanteuse,* starts humming a song which makes Jazz jump up and face the afternoon sky. Her arms are opened wide. She begins dancing in the middle of the empty lot, behind the train station. When the impromptu event concludes, we applaud our own talented team members who take a bow.

"You're quite in tune with each other, aren't you?" Stefan remarks, playfully with that crazy gu-gu-ga-ga enchanted look on his face.

Dahvid indicates it's time to continue.

"Shall we? Waterfall Kingdom awaits!" I proclaim. We walk on crunchy patches of pristine snow until we're told to stop. How odd, I'm okay with not knowing what's coming next. I can't help but stare at Josef and Stefan. They're so handsome and distinguished looking, dressed in their charcoal gray coats, so still and straight. They could easily pass for enchanted trees, guarding our forest. Dahvid and Sahrit are also bundled up. Does it get that cold in Dallas? They're wearing knit caps and… Wait— their woven scarves look like they're a coordinating set; same colors, different patterns, his has stripes, hers, swirls. Coincidence, I think not! Dahvid interrupts the colorful, geometric assessment, stating, "Take a look at the chart before you, it is at the core of TAP and how it functions."

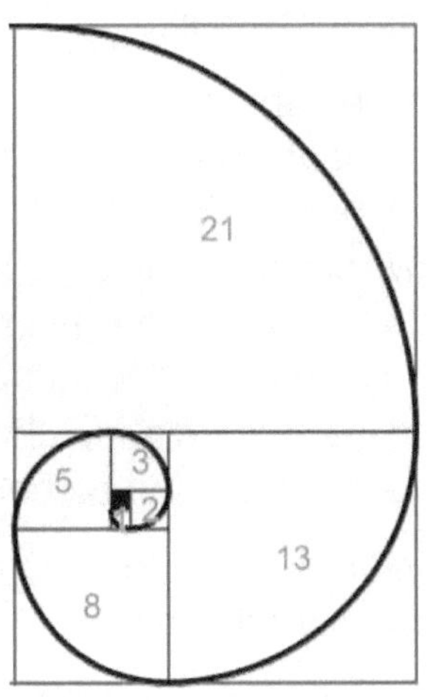

"It's the Fibonacci Spiral. You know that, right?" Tomas says with his tone. "Safe to say my mother is obsessed with it. It seems we have them everywhere. One which is framed, on the wall, looks centuries old. It's a technical drawing on parchment— Da Vinci style. It has formulas, calculations and various sketches."

"Why does your mother like it so much? Does it have anything to do with her line of work?" Stefan asks.

"Probably so— she's a scientist. I don't quite know what she does. Hard to believe, right?" he chuckles, awkwardly. "What I do know is that she works really hard, so I commissioned Jazz to create a special piece for Mom's birthday. What media was it again?"

"Diluted and texturized oils."

Since when does she mumble? Usually she'd go on and on about what inspired her to create her latest work of art. Ahh… bet she's nervous. No telling how or when Stefan's jealousy fest could make an appearance. Dahvid must be expecting a reaction too. "I would enjoy seeing the image and learn more about that technique. Will you share it with us sometime?"

Tomas jumps in, "We made a vid of the whole process, I can share it later."

He just stole Jazz's spotlight! Bleep! for him.

Stefan clears his throat a little too loudly and runs his hands nervously through his hair, making sure Jazz notices. We're all relieved by his mild reaction.

"What does the Spiral remind you of?" Dahvid asks Tomas.

"It may vary, depending on my state of mind. If I'm very agitated… maybe a cyclone. If I'm less agitated… a galaxy."

"Definitely a leaf unfurling for me!" I exclaim.

"Let me see…" Jazz says, tapping her upper lip. "It's a toss-up between a dancer's swirling skirt… or…. the twirl I make when I lick strawberry ice cream on a cone. What about you, Dahvid?" she asks flirtatiously.

"Since we're beginning this exciting journey together, I see a baby in its mother's womb… about to be born."

"That's sooo beautiful," she coos.

Sahrit follows, "I see the shape as pure essence. It contains all colors, all shapes, all patterns, and what may be beyond patterns. It provokes thoughts and evokes emotions. It's the shape of music as it leaves the instrument, travels through the air and enters the body to touch our soul."

Dahvid turns to her, "Sarita, that is absolutely magnificent."

Hmmm… that look he just gave her, he calls her Sarita, quite affectionate. The scarf thing and now this— they definitely have something going on. What a lucky girl! Chimes for me.

Stefan brings me back from my mental detour. "If you ask me, it looks like a black and white film I saw once, late at night. The kind where someone mysterious is looking down a spiral staircase from the top floor and plans to…"

"You mean a *Film Noir*? That genre is never inspiring, it's always dark, full of intrigue and aggression." Tomas remarks. Jazz picks up on his upset and tenses up.

Josef decides to move on, "A drone's view of the African continent… on a cloudless day."

Dahvid ties it all together, "Thank you all, for sharing your various perspectives. This exercise proves that The Fibonacci Spiral is around us and within us. It represents the beginning and the continuum of life."

"How— I— hate— hearing— that— phrase!" Tomas grunts, clenching his jaw. He raises both his fists up in the air. They're so tight, his knuckles turn bright white.

"*Perdón, amigo*. It had to be used in this context. *Respira*…" Dahvid remarks.

Tomas closes his eyes and follows the advice. He attempts deep breathing and then shakes the blood flow back into his hands. Jazz must know what's behind this extreme reaction. A couple of compassionate tears roll down her cheeks. I run my hand down her jacket's sleeve and give her a little smile. It's the only way to let her know that I feel badly for Tomas.

Our instructions continue. "We are going to work our way through a series of steps which will correlate with a series of ascending rates of accelerated time. With each stage in the series you will enter a different realm. Each realm will relate to different emotions and qualities."

Josef jumps in, "Whoa! You lost me after rates of acceleration— I'm not following. Esoteric stuff like that is way out of my league."

Did he just say esoteric? He's never used that word before. Are my signals and his crossing? Now that's really interesting…

"I've got a great sense of direction, but I'm totally lost, man," Stefan admits.

"This— right here— is exactly what makes us great as a team. We all learn and process information differently. The concrete thinkers offer a completely different perspective from those who can fully experience what is not present," Dahvid explains.

"Then there are those who can do both, like Ms. Ross, here," I add with a smile.

"Exactly. Now stay with me. I promise this will come together. But first, we need to release all negative or nervous energy so we can focus."

"Easier said than done. How do we do that?"

"Glad you asked, Tomas, move around, jump, jiggle, whatever you need to do to be still for the next sixty seconds," Dahvid clarifies.

"Okay, great, seems everyone is ready. Eyes closed, take a deep breath. Releeease… slowly," Dahvid instructs. "Stand up straight, arms by your sides, fingers extended, stay very still."

Asking me to be still is hard, but I will. I am.

"Good… now, keep your eyes closed until I say otherwise. We are about to begin our journey into TAP!"

I perceive vibrations in the ground and a series of soundless flashes that make me flinch, then it stops.

"Very slooowly… open your eyes…"

Jazz grabs my left arm then abruptly pulls away. "Ooops… sorry," she whispers and points. "Look at this gorgeousness!"

I can't focus on anything right now because of what I'm feeling or rather, not feeling. "The pain in my left arm is gone. It's totally gone." I whisper the incredible news in her ear. Teary-eyed, she takes my left hand and laces her fingers through it carefully.

Together, we take in the incredible scene. Our very familiar landscape has been overtaken by an enormous Fibonacci Spiral, hovering a few inches above the snow-covered ground. The shape's outlined in an indescribable color.

"Cool… so very cool, that's… my… balancing color," Tomas whispers to himself, knowing his secret is safe with us.

I'm so excited and nervous at the same time. "Are we about to be launched into space?"

"Can't wait to go wherever this ship is taking us," Jazz says, to which Sahrit adds, "I feel transported already."

How is it that Josef and Stefan say nothing? Guess they're awaiting further instructions.

The look on Dahvid's face is as indescribable as the color of this phenomenal spiral. "What an extraordinary work of art," he whispers.

It's thrilling to know we're all seeing this together and for the very first time.

"Everyone, step into the nucleus. It may look tight, but it will expand to fit us all. Please pay attention to the signage which will appear on the ground as you progress through it."

We step in and Dahvid announces, "Welcome

to the first sphere." As he extends his right hand, palm up, a beautiful little hummingbird flutters around him. He's enchanted. "Meet our beautiful and very talented new friend, Colibrí. She will be joining us on this journey."

The tiny bird shows off some fancy maneuvers mid-air.

"Make sure to watch her carefully as we transition through the different acceleration rates," Dahvid shares. Tomas is enthralled by the miniature, aerodynamic marvel.

"Oh my stars… she's poetry in motion," Sahrit sighs.

"Did you notice that her head matches your thermos— exactly! The contrast with the silvery gold of her body feathers, it's so gorgeous!" Jazz shares.

The magical creature completes her dance by hovering over Dahvid's fabulously lush, dark hair. I'm so grateful to Colibrí, now I can stare at him freely without being so obvious. Jazz covers her mouth with her hand and whispers, "*Bellisimo!*" Think she's also enjoying the great view. He explains that the series of directives were designed for each one of us. That no one else can see them and encourages us to take our time to work through them.

"To transition into the next ocular and audio function, blink twice— now!" he instructs.

A woman's kind voice welcomes me and instructs that I read, internalize and proceed.

"Step forward, please," the voice says. Writing hovers over the snow.

I read the paragraph once and try to step forward. The tiny bird moves backwards and forward, in place. I read it again, same thing happens. After my third attempt, the words 'Chromo Enhancer Activated' appear and colors shift, including Colibrí's. The drab looking winter panorama comes alive, bathed in every possible green. The tiny bird turns emerald. I feel calm and balanced. I go to the next stop.

This is also extremely challenging. I read it several times. Colibrí dashes around in a cheery new costume, picking up soft yellows. A fragrant dash of lemongrass presents itself. I need more time to process this, but my guide thinks differently. I move to the next stop.

This is monumental. Kindness and strength, together? I've always been so afraid to show kindness for fear of appearing weak and vulnerable. Guess I overdeveloped that muscle preparing for debates, I couldn't lose control. Colibrí shimmers before me, dressed in a golden gown. The aroma and the warmth of caramel melt on some of the lemony yellows. My tiny companion seems to be slowing down, must be so I can appreciate her figure eight wing movements. Her effort is leaving frozen little trails shaped like eternity symbols. I step forward.

Urgently need to acquire this one. It's time to be brave in a whole new way by breaking through this thick protective cocoon. Colibrí celebrates my keen observations by slipping into coral attire. The refreshing subtlety of grapefruit washes over me.

Desperately want this one, too. I really struggle putting others' needs before mine. The chromo enhancer is becoming less noticeable. Is the sun is setting? I've lost track of time. Colibrí agrees by waltzing in, wearing a deep purple gown. I'm surprised by the luxury of lavender.

Major struggle with giving. I need to learn how to be more comfortable expressing my feelings. Can't expect those around me to be telepathic and accommodating. By getting a handle on Gentility and Grace, I'll be able to express love more openly. Colibrí transitions into the intensity of blue. I'm allowed to move forward.

Would I lose Humility points if I dared to describe myself as a visionary? Colibrí gets very close. Is it possible that I can see her tiny, little eyes looking straight at me? Do birds smile? She takes on a series of still-shot, ballet-like poses, that if strung together would show that she's spinning joyfully. Once she stops, her delicate little body is dusted, head to tail, by iridescent turquoise. She looks just like Dahvid's mysterious vessel. Does this little creature nourish his gentility with sweet nectars, collected from invisible flowers grown in other dimensions? These thoughts can't possibly be mine. They sound like lyrics in one of Sahrit's songs.

Wait— why was there no flavor or scent attached to the last two velocities? As I ponder on possibilities for Love and Vision, a new message hovers over the snow:

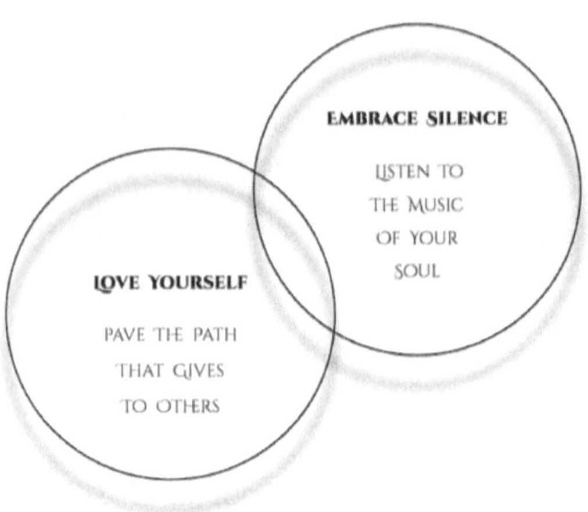

Why do I feel like laughing and crying at the same time? I'll have to sort that out in the near future. Dahvid is speaking in the here and now.

We're instructed to close our eyes again and remain still for the next sixty seconds. Interesting… this time, I don't feel the need to shake stuff off. If anything, I want to retain everything inside. Wait— am I floating? It's as if my feet have left the ground…

The distant sound of the early evening mockingbirds help me return to Planet Earth.

Dahvid's shares the next set of instructions, "Your eyes need to remain closed. What you are experiencing is known as Serenity."

This feels absolutely wonderful. Wonder how long we can stay?

"On the count of three— inhale as deeply as you can and snap your fingers four times. Excellent! You have now activated the system that allows you to capture The Fibonacci Experience. Your mind, body and soul have retained the information. You can replay and relive it, at will, any time, including thoughts, emotions and sensory responses. To test its efficacy, in a moment I will prompt you to snap your fingers three times, so you can review it all of it or only portions. If you activate this experience daily, it will ensure being fully absorbed within you. More steps will be added."

There's still more? I can't possibly process any more. "Snap!" Dahvid commands.

The rerun begins and I see what I had seen, read what I had read, hear what I had heard. I question all my questions and doubt all my doubts. Upon completion, I open my eyes, realizing that I no longer fear some fears and I'm ready to feel some of my feelings.

Dahvid appears to radiate like the sun. "On behalf of the entire team, we…" he stops and takes a deep breath.

He isn't reaching for… There's no thermos… Wonder if he overcame the need for it?

He proceeds, "Please, take a moment to thank your inner essence for being open and vulnerable. That was the ticket you needed to present at the gate to enter this spectacular life-altering experience. As of this evening, we have bonded with ourselves and with each other in a deep way. We are now prepared to enter a whole new dimension, with a new awareness and new responsibilities."

He's on the verge of tears and so am I. Who would ever think of thanking oneself for anything? I'm always so busy telling others or myself what to do or not do. I'm always busy thinking how to fix or solve things. But, after this, I get it— I need to start by repairing all the misdeeds I've inflicted upon others and myself. How can I possibly aspire to repair the world, otherwise? Wow… was that insight or intuition? Whatever it is, I love it! Uh… ohhh… I just missed the beginning of Leonardo's message that Dahvid is reading.

"The tools you have acquired today shall serve you for life. This metamorphosis represents a new era, one of liberation for superhumans. What we will accomplish together is no longer within the realm of the unimaginable. Congratulations to all of you and now…"

Dahvid stops to point at the evening sky with one hand, as he wipes his tears with the other.

"Wowowow! This is beyond the beyond spectacular!" I exclaim. Without thinking, my arms extend straight up, forming a giant 'V'. It's as if my body instinctively needs to create a funnel to receive this experience. I turn in all directions, taking in the incredible sites. Above us is a densely colored cloud, filled with bioluminescent creatures adding to the thousands of sparkles in the crisp night sky.

Tomas interjects, "Their presence is a virtual metaphor for what we just experienced. You know they're not real, right?"

"What do you mean they're not real? Look at them!" I exclaim.

"It's an illusion, Jess. Everybody knows that butterflies can't fly when it's this cold— nor at night!" he explains in his pedantic tone.

"Oh Tomas... I wish you hadn't..." Jazz expresses her grand dismay.

"What's the difference?" Stefan cuts in.

"It makes a huge difference!" she responds, quite annoyed.

"That's it!" Tomas yells out, stunning the colorful cloud. It freezes in motion and their light dims. "I just realized why my mother stopped taking me to live performances when I was younger. She taught us how to manage our money wisely, so I always thought we were short on funds. That wasn't it at all. We stopped going because I kept interrupting and explaining everything that was going on, especially technical trickery. I couldn't help myself, seems I still can't."

Jazz and Sahrit touch their hearts. Poor Tomas Kesher, he looks like a blow-up figure, loosing air, flattening slowly to the ground.

Sweet Sahrit comes to the rescue, "As a performer, I'm involved in all aspects of what goes into producing a show. We work really hard so that things run seamlessly. Our goal is for the audience to get lost in the experience. Dahvid's team has worked extremely hard to present us with this stupendously groovy happening. Let's thank them by getting back into it. Shall we?"

Tomas and Stefan both agree, allowing the butterflies to start moving and glowing once again. Their light divulges Dahvid's somewhat disappointed expression. Is he upset because Tomas interrupted the show?

The flickering cloud starts separating into groups that descend upon us, allowing a closer look at their colorful beauty. They surround each one of us like fluttering columns, in constant motion. Through a tiny gap, I get a glimpse of Jazz.

Look at her, she's in her element. Rejoicing magentas are kissing her cheeks, nose, and lips. Little pinks flit around her head, adding movement to the stones on her plastique tiara, which remains firmly attached to her swirly-twirly, cinnamon hair. I wish she could see what I'm seeing. Wonder if anyone is looking at me? The answer comes in the form of two butterflies. They land, one on each of my lids, forcing me to close my eyes, signaling, "Stay in the moment."

Seconds later, the fluttering messengers take off, allowing me to see what's happening. They've regrouped and perched around the entire perimeter of the Fibonacci Spiral. Amazing how it continues to hover above the sparkling snow-covered ground. Monarchs use their rich orange, black and white wings to help lift the heavy piece onto its side. The rest of the colorful crew joins in and levels the large structure in the air. They fly off and it all disappears in the dark, velvety-blue sky.

Dahvid still in a state of awe, whispers, "That was the most breathtaking thing I have ever seen."

Jazz lets out a big sigh, "Dreamy beyond all the dreamiest of dreams."

"Remarkable!" comes from Tomas.

"Indescribable! Thank you, Leonardo and everyone who made this event possible. It's exciting to know that with your tech, we'll retain this through our senses. Can't wait to replay it when I get home!" I exclaim.

"Did you know it's been scientifically proven that if one captures an event on a device, the emotional attachment is nonexistent?" Tomas remarks. "That's why it's important to be present in the moment. I may understand it in theory but struggle with it in realty."

Wait— we have that in common, too? Interesting how Tomas became comfortable enough to share his thoughts and feelings. Not me— not yet— not all— no way!

The thought leaves my mind when I hear Dahvid suggesting we head home. He's not a fan of the cold, and temps are dropping quickly in Dallas. "Fifty minutes will give me enough time to escort Sahrit home and catch up with some work and meet again."

As I lock arms with Jazz, Tomas decides to walk next to me, an unexpected change.

We reach Jazz's home. The side entrance takes us into their super cool kitchen. It could pass for a cafe in a sophisticated hotel in the city. Using their Glåsse, I keep my promise and call Mom.

"That must have been quite an elevating journey, you remembered to call! Thank you. Let me know when you leave, please."

"Mooom, I'm across the street!" I quickly reconsider. "Yes, ma'am, that makes sense."

Jazz gives me two thumbs up and asks with a British accent, "May I get my honored guests anything to eat or drink?"

"Hot chocolate and scones?" Tomas requests.

"Excellent idea, sir. And you, Ms. Stafford?"

"That sounds perfectly delightful," I say, removing my gloves and rubbing warmth into my cold hands. I don't dare remove my cap, otherwise, my hair will shoot straight up and poke the ceiling. Practicing how to share vulnerability, I turn to Tomas, point at the cap and say, "I'll keep it on. Static… you know?"

Rubbing his hair and making it flare out like a peacock's tail, Tomas replies, "I do."

Jazz announces, "Deluxe Chocoliciousness A La Rossé— coming up!" She reaches for three oversized mugs and lines them up on the counter. While we wait, she gives us paper napkins with funky designs and edible mocha spoons. "Sorry, we seem to be fresh out of scones but we do have fresh whipped cream, mini-mallows, pecans, chocolate and caramel syrup." The royal accent continues.

Tomas receives his warm frothy mug, holds it with both hands, sighs deeply and shares, "I need to apologize for ruining the show for you— and everybody, for that matter."

Jazz says nothing, giving me the opening to

respond. "We value your vast scientific and tech knowledge, Tomas, really— we do. To be honest, I admit that at first... I was upset you interrupted, but now— I'm actually grateful."

"You're grateful I interrupted? That's a first..."

"It frustrated me but that was a good sign."

"But I frustrate you a lot and that never seems to be a good sign."

"That's because this time I wasn't frustrated with you. I was upset because I couldn't get lost in the moment. Isn't that just fantastic?"

"I guess?" He tilts his head like a puppy, totally perplexed.

"That's super great news, Jess, congrats!" Jazz exclaims.

I just shared something personal that made me vulnerable and... I'm okay. Chimes for me. I celebrate by taking a sip of hot chocolate and give them a little shy smile. Tomas points at me and starts laughing.

"Hey! What's so funny?"

"Since you appreciate my interruptions, here's another one— there's cream on your nose."

"No there's not!" I snap back, with familiar annoyance towards him. The feeling goes away when Sahrit shows up.

"I'm so happy to see you!" I exclaim with relief.

She taps the tip of her nose and winks. I reach for my napkin. Grrr… I didn't just have cream but syrup, too. That's enough embarrassment.

"Perfect timing, Sahrit, we were just admiring Jess's nose, I mean— Jazz's tabletop." Tomas quips. Smooth way of changing the subject.

"What is that material, anyway?" Sahrit asks, trying to inspect the surface.

"Splendoriffic, isn't it? It has a connection to the cosmos," Jazz responds.

"Yes, it is! Those coppery, golden flecks look like stars in the heavens," Sahrit responds.

Josef, Stefan, and Dahvid join us, so Jazz decides to include them in the brief geological explanation about the material. All I have the energy to capture is that it's known as Black Galaxy and it's found in India.

Dahvid lets us know that after he dropped Sahrit off, he realized he omitted something very important about Colibrí.

"Let me guess… we each get our own and a set of coordinating butterflies as graduation presents?" Jazz remarks.

"Impossible, she happens to be one of a kind." He pauses for a moment and then adds, "Tomas, do you know what was left out?"

"Yes, I do, but you go ahead. This is your

presentation," he responds graciously.

"Obviously, there was a lot to take in earlier, but do you remember I asked that you watch her closely? Did anyone notice the chromo filters and the variances in her movements?"

"I did but I didn't say anything because I thought I was losing it," Stefan remarks, brushing through his hair, looking relieved.

"What color filters?" Josef turns to him, looking quite puzzled.

Wait— Josef isn't colorblind. He, of all people would be aware of every single thing going. Can't believe he missed something I caught. Now, more than ever, wish I had access to his hue.r.u. Jazz picks up her edible spoon and twirls it around making figure eights in the air. That prompts Dahvid to explain. "It was not that Colibrí was slowing down— we were accelerating. As in we caught up with her."

Trying humility on for size, I remark, "Now that you mention it, I do recall seeing the colors and the change of speed."

Dahvid smiles and exhales deeply, "Excellent! Believe it or not, we have— finally— reached the most important part of today's meeting."

"Finally? Are you kidding me? What else is there?" Stefan remarks, sounding fed up.

"The matter is highly confidential, I will try to be

brief. Our group has managed to infiltrate a portion of the WLC's internal communication system and…"

I bang both my hands on the Black Galaxy and exclaim, "Tomas— you knew, didn't you? Jazz said you were upset yesterday morning, right before the WLC announcement."

Tomas becomes very twitchy and bites down, much too hard on his edible spoon. Myriads of mocha bits fly off everywhere.

"To be fair, Tomas was made privy only to some classified information, but not all of it," Dahvid clarifies.

"You must have really impressive credentials, man," Stefan compliments him, but Tomas ignores it. His energy is focused on containing an interplanetary mocha cleanup mission.

Dahvid continues, "As I was saying, for our future endeavors to succeed, we need to have much greater access to the WLC and The Chancellor, himself."

"But how?" I ask, leaning forward.

"It requires installing highly advanced tech, with a slight caveat: it has to be done in person."

"Slight caveat? Seriously, Dahvid? Who in the world would want to do such a crazy thing? It's way too dangerous!" I exclaim.

"In person is the only way. The process is exactly as the one you experienced, someone applies the drops for someone else."

"But we were all aware of each other!" Sahrit exclaims with a shaky voice.

"That is because we were all moving at the same accelerated rate. Whoever takes this on would be in TAP where The Chancellor would remain in real time. With proper training there is no danger of being discovered. We would be able to preempt The Chancellor's every move!" Dahvid clarifies.

"Are you saying… we'd see what he sees… hear what he hears and says?" Jazz asks.

Tomas smiles and nods.

"First of all— yuck! Second, who wants to get that close to him? The thought of it makes me sick," Jazz remarks, making an unpleasantly funny face.

"Would you consider… me for this mission?"

"Whaaat?" I yell out. "Josef Tallon-Saldane, are you absolutely crazed out of your very sensible mind? You don't know what this entails, it's way too dangerous! I'm in charge of this group, and I say— no, absolutely not!" I turn to Dahvid for support who looks thrilled… Really? Joy? At a time like this?

Josef's never looked happier. He explains that

if he were to be accepted, being part of a mission of this magnitude would be a dream come true. It would make his life worthwhile. It would finally have purpose.

Jazz stands up, taking her turn at hitting the tabletop, palms down. "Excuuuse me! You have a purposeful life, already! What do you call the outstanding job you've done looking after your younger brother?"

"Oh man— she's right," Stefan remarks. "I just realized… I've never thanked you. I've only taken from you and what you've done for me— for granted. I've been riding on you my whole life. You've given me so much, especially confidence. But— who's looked after you? What do you need from me?"

Josef tries to answer, but can't say a word.

"Big Bro… Will you ever forgive me?" Stefan pleads.

Jazz's eyes produce tears the size of pearls. They roll down her cheeks and pierce through the thick whipped cream in her mug.

Josef struggles to contain a lifetime of pent up emotions. The dam finally breaks, he opens those strong arms and hugs his brother. No kid should have to parent a sibling. Josef has. This is a defining moment. They're finally free to express their thoughts and feelings. I'm so happy for them that I could burst. But if I did, I'd spray multi-colored confetti all over and I'd be cleaning for days. The image adds giggles to my tears.

Stefan pulls away from his brother, and wipes his eyes with his coat sleeves. He clears his throat and announces, "A tech implanting mission such as this is considered extremely dangerous. It requires a great deal of planning and coordination between operatives. I would like to volunteer to support my brother!"

"Oh, Stefan!" Jazz exclaims, bursting into tears. Guessing she's overcome by fear and pride— I know I am.

Dahvid uses the multi-colored, striped knit scarf, draped around his neck, to pat his eyes. "Gentlemen, thank you! As far as we are concerned, no one could be better suited for… one moment, please." He pauses to listen to a separate audio. "Sorry about that… Your dedication and loyalty are exemplary. I was just informed that a major donor has contributed a sizable amount towards our initiative. Junior Cadets Josef and Stefan Tallon-Saldane, we thank you for your dedication and bravery." Dahvid salutes them.

Tomas rubs his hands, nervously, "Wish I could do more, but I'm not exactly known for my talent at applying drops, nor graceful moves, especially around chairs. The last thing we need is for something to go seriously wrong."

"Before the tech implementation can take place, our military team needs specialized training and be fitted for full body, protective garments," Dahvid clarifies.

"What are the garments made of?" Our curious fashionista wants to know.

"Great question. What is the most polyfacetic material available?"

"Graphene?" she remarks with a hopeful tone.

"Correct! Since their experience will be much like a rocket re-entering the atmosphere, they will need to be shielded from the friction and heat generated by traveling at extremely high speeds. The protective gear is designed to provide a cooling system, which balances any thermal variances and is able to block sonic disturbances."

Tomas questions their mode of transportation and the speed they'd attain. Dahvid explains, "They will be using a type of hovering scooter, capable of reaching up to 10,000 miles per hour. Sahrit, as a conservationist, you will appreciate knowing that there are no sonic disturbances, nor damage to the environment."

"There is much more to cover, but it will be part of your training. So gentlemen, shall we?" The brothers salute, making no effort to contain their excitement. The three guys slowly blur out of sight and disappear.

"Hope he's only training them— for now. I couldn't possibly process one more emotion today— I'm completely spent," Jazz declares.

Tomas chimes in, "Don't count on it— if they go back into TAP, the training and the mission could happen between heartbeats."

"Don't even go there, please!" Jazz exclaims, covering her face.

To create a much-needed distraction, Sahrit decides to share her ideas for this weekend's concert. We're so absorbed in the details, that we don't pick up when Dahvid's back.

"Did I miss much?" Dahvid jokes.

"Where are they? Are they okay?" I ask.

"They are already involved in our mission." Dahvid responds, calmly. "Hold on— Josef and Stefan have something to share."

A scene slowly materializes in front of us. Looking disheveled, a man in his forties is struggling with a gray lab coat. It's inside out. Orange-rimmed glasses and pale tinted lenses make him look like a cartoon character.

"What may I do for you today?" he asks.

The World Chancellor's dreaded voice replies, "Doctor Kuracanto, you know my physiology better than I do. I have a big problem, and you need to resolve it!" he proclaims.

"What seems to be the problem?"

"Something is wrong— very, very wrong. I demand to know what it is— immediately!"

The World Chancellor describes a series of discomforts, that developed out of nowhere, just minutes ago. It all seems to have started with giggling that progressed to laughter.

"Why is that a problem, Your Excellency? Laughing is a healthy response to something or someone that causes amusement or better yet— joy."

We see The Chancellor outstretching his arm, revealing that he's wearing that disgusting gray with skin tight gloves to match. I feel sick. He bangs on his desk, everything rattles.

"I cannot tolerate the sound of anyone's laughter, let alone, my own! The way I feel right now is far from joyful. The subcutaneous itching is escalating, as we speak. I am experiencing severe burning— everywhere! Do you hear me? Everywhere! I demand answers— at once! This is unbearable!"

"I will do my best, Your Excellency," the doctor responds nervously, loosening the already crooked knot in his orange and gray striped tie. He finds it impossible to reason with his stubborn patient, who refuses to touch his own skin and scratch directly for relief. The eccentric man reminds the doctor why he requires wearing gloves and special clothing at all times. He insists on protecting himself not only from the elements, but from bacteria, viruses, and who knows what else.

The Chancellor moves on to ask, "I also need to know what in the blazes is— thiiss?"

The doctor looks surprised and with a shaky voice, responds, "It is best not to speculate until we have more information, Your Excellency. Once we run a complete set of internal and external tests, we will be able to discuss our findings."

"You cannot tell me now? Are you saying I must tolerate this agony longer?"

"Respectfully, sir, without tests we are unable to give you answers. Our system has to retrofit information for someone in, shall we say, your unique circumstances. We cannot make any assumptions. Normally, we'd ask that you place your bare hand on the screen. In this case, we will do our best through Iridology and Facial Dermal analysis. Please try not to blink for 10 seconds."

"Are we done here?"

"I need ten seconds, sir," the doctor repeats.

The Ogre responds by banging with both fists, "Eight seconds should be more than enough. As it is, I'm giving you a very generous thirty minutes to resolve my medical emergency. Not a moment longer!" he barks and bangs.

The doctor tries to remain calm and changes the subject, "Please study this list of homeopathic remedies, for topical use only. Like most people, you should have these ingredients in your kitchen."

"How dare you equate me with most people! Leave now! Thirty minutes, not a nanosecond longer!" he demands.

The nervous man, who's been sweating the entire time, bows to be excused and the cartoonish spectacles slide off his face. The image breaks down into orange, black and white pixels which transform into the recipes.

Through The Chancellor's eyes, we see him reviewing the options to prepare pastes and soaking compounds. He focuses on a variety of chilled alcohol compresses. He gets up, walks a few steps and makes an exaggerated sharp right turn. We hear his *flamenco* heels on the hard floor.

"Thaaat's— his— kitchen?" Jazz whispers, looking shocked.

"It looks more like a safety chamber in a radioactive facility to me," Tomas replies.

The chancellor opens a vertical cabinet, with top shelves no higher than his eye level. It's filled with soaps, disinfectants of all sorts and paper products. Wham! He slams the cabinet door in frustration. The next cabinet he opens, contains every possible type of drinking glass imaginable. He scans over the most delicate, cut crystal, little goblets to the clunkiest tumblers that must weigh half a ton.

"Stupendous! I knew I'd have containers for the most effective remedy." He selects the two largest, tallest, cylindrical glasses he owns, sets them on a concrete surface. He gently drops five ice cubes in each, counting one at a time. From a locked cabinet, he retrieves two liquor bottles that show '190 proof' on the label. The contents are poured, simultaneously, to the brim, into each of the glasses. He walks back to the desk, positions the heavy glasses on thick, gray stone coasters and sits.

"My dear Kuracanto, you expect me to waste such a fine remedy on cold compresses? Why rub it on if you can drink it?" he declares, loudly— to no one. He holds one glass in each of his sickly, pasty, gray hands.

Clink! "Nostrovia!" The toast bounces, over and over, creating the illusion that others, who are definitely not there, echo the sentiments in his sterile environment. The vibrations awaken the oversized monitor, showing numerous split screens. He taps on one, and in a surprisingly juvenile voice, says, "It's Marvelous Maarlee!"

He reviews the titles of all her shows and watches some snippets, alternating gulps of his chilled remedies until they're gone.

"Now… this is going to be even mooore fun!" he exclaims, sounding even more childlike.

"Nooo! Stop! That's impossible!" I scream.

The connection cuts off.

Dahvid gets on his private line, trying to decipher what happened, all while I'm bombarding him with screaming questions. Tomas is rocking and shaking, Jazz is hugging herself, Sahrit is whimpering, curled like a ball.

When the conversation ends, he clasps his hands together, begging us for the impossible.

"How can we be calm? Who knows how long His Wickedness has been on Liberty World!" I yell out.

"In an effort to protect the members of your communication platform, Josef and Stefan were able to cut off his access, but it may be only temporarily," Dahvid explains and then excuses himself, he's needed urgently.

Jazz is very upset, trying to explain through breathless sobs, "Jess… I swear… it's impossible… for anyone… to break through."

"I believe you… he's a ruthless monster… he respects no one… he'll stop at nothing…"

"He has a dark side… he takes pleasure… in destroying… especially truth… and light," Sahrit whispers through sobs.

"He's everything you say he is, plus he's an energy vampire!" Tomas shouts out. His face turns bright red, the veins in his neck pop out.

With that we stop speaking until Sahrit is calm enough to suggest we do deep breathing exercises.

"Wish I could but I just can't. I can't let go of the furry and the fear," I explain, noticing that Tomas isn't doing so well, either.

Sahrit gets on the floor and starts reciting, slowly and softly, "We are vibration… we are sound… we are light… we are color… we are shape… we are hope…"

Jazz joins in and after the third repetition, their faces and bodies are noticeably relaxed. They 'return' calm and start talking, as if they were already involved in the conversation. Do they have telepathy with each other?

"Jazz, so where did you say you got those oversized mugs? They're totally fabulicious! Do you know if they carry matching plates and bowls? I want the whole set!" Sahrit remarks.

"I just make them and paint them… for fun."

Getting on board with their potentially telepathic, creative wave, I come up with an idea on raising money for our initiative. "Jazz, could you design a tableware line with a 1970's psychedelic vibe? It could be presented as a limited edition, endorsed and autographed by none other than our songbird, Sahrit Bana."

"What a groovy idea, I'm in!" Sahrit exclaims. "Jessica Stafford, you leave me no choice but to dub thee, Mastermind and Top Visionary. You have such a way of anticipating what the public wants. Like our other ventures, this is going to be a big hit— I can feel it! This will help our talented friend make a name for herself as an artist." She turns to Jazz, "You're so talented, I'm happy to endorse it but you'll be signing the collection. The recognition belongs to you!"

Jazz smiles, closes her eyes and fresh, happy tears roll down her lovely face. She deserves support from someone as generous and thoughtful as she is. This must qualify as a Zivah Zahav moment…

Witnessing the special moment, helps Tomas calm down. "Consider taking this a step further. Sell mugs and bowls of different sizes filled with sealed, pre-measured ingredients. That would provide an opportunity to up-sell."

"Ingredients for what?" I ask.

"This hot chocolate crazy-good concoction, or chunky soups, or single serving cakes, or…"

He stops talking, because I'm staring at him in

shock. "Tomas Kesher, first I find out you're a gifted broker, then a musician, and now a marketing foodie, too?"

"Shaaring time," Jazz suggests melodiously.

"But you know I abhor braggers," he snaps.

"You're not bragging at all, you're simply stating facts, just like with the butterflies. Go for it!"

He takes a deep breath. "Okay… My mom, Maddy, and I have a catering business. It's called Food For Thought. It started small, at home, but then my extroverted sister decided to tell the whole world about it," he pauses trying to keep calm. "Long story short, we outgrew the kitchen so we had to expand. We're in a food industry, shared space. That's where production, assembly, and distribution happens. Bottom line… if you want… we can help."

"I'm speechless…" I quip.

"By the way, their food is scrumptiously delicious. Tomas and his mom develop all the recipes themselves. They have a la carte items or full course menus," Jazz adds.

"Have you published a cookbook yet?" Sahrit inquires.

"Guessing my answer needs to be… not yet?"

"Have you noticed that today keeps getting

better and better? I propose a toast!" Sahrit suggests and goes off camera. She zips back, holding a fancy champagne flute with four maraschino cherries. They bobble, happily as the sparkling water is poured over them.

"To new lives, new ventures, and hope for the future!" she declares. Tomas and I raise our soon-to-be famously decorated mugs as Jazz follows by saying, "*Santé, mes amis!*"

"*Salud, dinero y amor!*" comes from Dahvid.

"Everything okay?" I ask nervously.

"Honestly, no, not quite, but let us focus on the future. Shall we? Your ideas are superb. Our group can help with this too by creating code for mass production via Klôner. All we need is a prototype for each piece, they will do the rest. The products will appear just like these, handmade, with slightly irregular shapes, raised brush strokes, whatever you want."

"This is so super exciting. I know I'll be up all night, drawing and coloring!" Jazz exclaims.

"This is undisputedly, a Zivah Zahav moment," I mumble.

"Jess, did you say something?" Sahrit asks.

I shake my head, smile and say, "Just happy."

Sahrit plops a fifth cherry to her flute, "Ladies and gentlemen, to The Fab Five!"

"Sorry, to interrupt— we're reconnecting." Dahvid announces. The timer shows that twenty-eight and a half minutes have passed since Dr. Kuracanto pixilated into recipes.

"Your Excellency, thank you for your infinite patience, I have some information for you."

The all too familiar gravelly voice is slurring, "Are you going to tell me… what in the blazes… happened with my monitor?"

"Sir?"

"Never mind! Do you have the diagnosis? Quickly! What is wrong with me? The remedy is wearing off, I don't have all day!" he pushes, in a drunken stupor.

"It seems…"

"Get on with it, man!" he barks.

"…that there are unidentifiable substances circulating in your body."

"You and I both know that's absolutely impossible!" The Chancellor hits the desk with both fists, making the two large, empty glasses fall and shatter on the floor. "I live in extreme isolation 98% of the time. The daily hyperbaric chamber session should prevent any other unexpected exposure. I am the only person on Earth who doesn't have nano implants. You are the authority on anti-nano technology and forensics. How hard can this be?"

"Your Excellency… you may not be the only person on Earth without implants. There may be others…"

"Absolutely ridiculous! There is no one else like me on the planet!" he insists. The Chancellor is too drunk to notice that the doctor is struggling to keep a straight face. "What about this thing under my right eye?"

The doctor clears his throat to respond, "Some, not all, of the unknown substances seem to have been introduced through the eyes. We believe that an infinitesimal amount spilled out when you blinked. Once it came in contact with the air, the fluid crystallized, leaving a blue, tear-shaped, dermal imprint."

He bangs again, "I have trained my physiology not to produce tears. I will not be associated with emotion or weakness of any kind. Do you hear me? Can you imagine how that would affect my image as The World Dictator— I mean Chancellor? I'd lose all credibility!"

"I understand your predicament, sir. We can arrange for a procedure to have It removed."

"Absolutely not! Nobody— I mean nobody, comes anywhere near me from now on!"

The tremulous Dr. Kuracanto arranges his skewed orange spectacles and fidgets with his inside out lab coat.

"Being that we have identified foreign matter, your case requires a completely different battery of tests."

The Chancellor bangs so hard on his desk that the monitor jumps. Dr. Kuracanto tries to ignore what just happened, and asks, "Sir, which of the holistic remedies worked best?"

"I don't… seem… to recall… now," he slurs.

"When you do remember, you may apply it as often as needed. Do I have your approval to run more tests through an IVP laboratory?"

"Doctor, I'm losing the last ounce of patience I had left over from last week! Get it straight— you mean a VIP laboratory. Of course, who better to oversee my case?"

"Sir, IVP means Intergalactic Viral Programs."

"Whaaat? Are you saying I have…? Arrange for the IVP testing immediately!" his voice cracks like a scared boy.

The doctor's tone changes to make a point, "Sir, their protocol is such that one may request their assistance, it is up to them to decide who or what takes priority."

"How dare you insinuate that my health is not top priority! Who is the man in charge of this so called Inter… whatever group?"

Dr. Kuracanto, takes a deep breath and

responds in a slow and deliberate manner, "Your Excellency… the person in charge has top clearance. Dare I say, the most brilliant, accomplished scientist I have ever known."

"That is the first piece of good news you have given me all day. Tell me, then— what is the best method of persuasion to get my name at the top of the list?"

"Your Excellency, this is a remarkable person, someone with the utmost degree of integrity and unmatched work ethic…"

The Ogre uses a fake, kind tone to say, "Face it, Kuracanto, everyone has a price. You did. Now— give me his name at once!" he bangs.

"The highly distinguished and world-renowned scientist I'm referring to is…. forgive me for saying this, Your Excellency, is not man."

The Chancellor gets up and reaches for his oversized gavel. Instead of banging over and over with it, like he did at the WLC, he stares at it. He holds it with both hands squinting, making sure it's perfectly parallel to the desk. He grunts and in one move— snaps the rod in half, sending large splintered pieces of red and yellow painted wood, flying everywhere.

Simultaneously, the shelves behind the doctor shake, causing a collection of apothecary jars, to crack. The contents— different colored fluids, begin oozing out. Dr. Kuracanto's office is filling with thick, brown smoke making it harder to see him. He's coughing, chocking. The Chancellor, oblivious to the situation, yells out, "I despise dealing with women in any capacity! There must be a male that is head of the department. Who is it? Tell me!"

He gasps for air to say, "Dr. Paula Kesher… Your Excellency, is the head of the entire…."

Jazz screams out, "Help! Mommy! Daddy! Help! Emergency! Tomas just fainted!"

CAST

Jessica Stafford
Josef Tallon Saldane
Dahvid Toledano
Tomas Kesher
Jasmin Ross
Maarlee McGee
Sahrit Bana
Mia & Uriel Toledano
Stefan Tallon Saldane

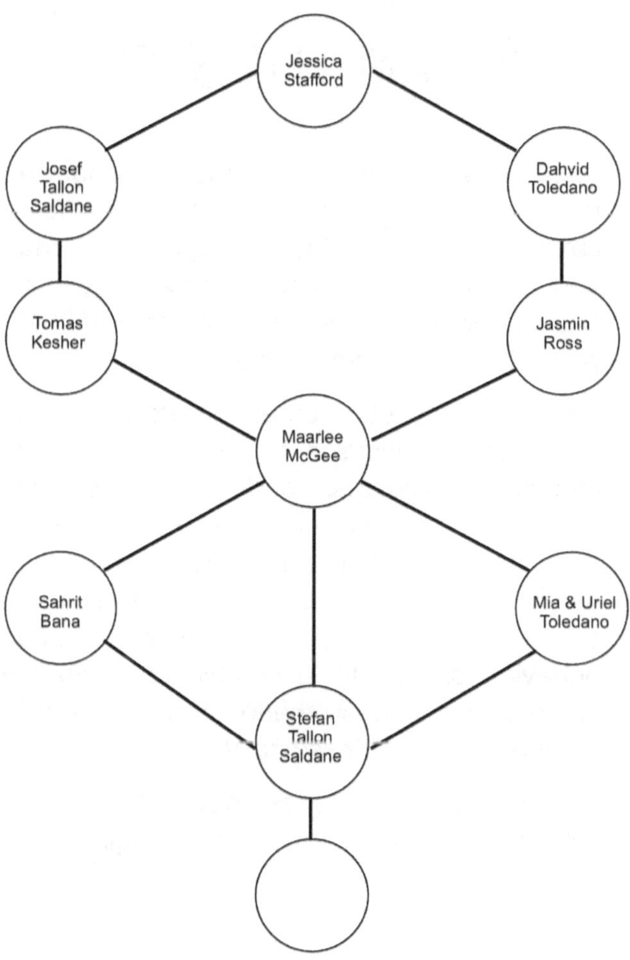

A STORY...
WITHIN THE STORY

Within days, Carolyn and Robert recognized they were designed for each other. They felt a connection often seen in movies and read about in books. It was as if they already knew each other but, it was until December of 2017, when they finally met in person.

They validated each other's impressions and challenges of living in the world as creative introverts, empaths, and highly sensitive people in a world run by extroverts. Their combined interests in art, architecture, design, music, technology, literature, theatre, cinema, biology, archeology, anthropology, human behavior, spirituality in combination with the same sense humor, made them a great fit, personally and professionally.

As in all great love stories, they both got much more than they ever would have imagined.

About the Authors...

ROBERT GOLD, once a telecommunication systems sales executive and owner of an electrical contracting business has been forever learning and exploring. He became fascinated by the relatively unknown field of ontology which combines architecture, anthropology, neuro and cellular biology. With years of study and practice, he has transformed many lives and has developed accounting systems which support the growth of successful businesses.

For a number of years, while head coaching human development coaches, he continued exploring his own life. Through that process, the visionary and inventor emerged from within, as did an intuitive system which could be the next logical step after the Internet. This concept could improve methods of communication while expanding the capacity for greater privacy. Robert determined that if feelings and emotions were to be connected to colors and body sensations, we could improve our self-awareness.

The scientific basis for his invention is found in Dwelling In A New World, where he concludes that tech driven synesthesia will be available in a not-so-distant future. Liberty 2041 features his inventions as part of the everyday lives of the characters.

CAROLYN FEDER GOLD, a classically trained interior designer, worked for a couple of large design firms most of her career until she founded her own business in 2008. By discovering that her unique perceptions of the world were enhanced by the 'gift' of synesthesia, everything in her life and in her practice, changed. Based on her own experiences and backed by scientific research, Carolyn had much to share. She created innovative methods to help her clients live better lives by making their environments more effective from a sensory standpoint. For years now, her unique practice has focused on peoples' wellbeing, especially children, by combining her field with science. Her clients have included practitioners in various therapeutic fields as well as children and adults on the autism spectrum.

One of her dreams had been to write a book that would express the many dimensions of color, light, form and texture and their effects from her unique point of view. How to convey it all eluded her until she met Robert Gold and read the original manuscript for the Liberty 2041 Series.

'IN HIS OWN WORDS...

Blessed with a precocious nature, growing up in Dallas made me feel constantly judged and misunderstood. During difficult times, climbing trees, especially the one in my front yard, gave me solace and the inner strength to persevere. To this day, studying a tree's majesty and sharing what makes some ideal for climbing gives me great pleasure.

What I knew and accomplished as a toddler, defied all explanation, I was much too young to follow written instructions. But once I started reading, I couldn't stop, specifically when it came to Albert Einstein. Finally, I had met another brilliant, misunderstood child to identify with. He became my earliest male role model. Aside from pondering about the mysteries of the universe, I was also a very active little boy who enjoyed playing outside with friends.

Throughout my life, I have found that instinct has always directed me towards truth over falsehood and light over darkness. What better example than Faith Leicht (pronounced *light*) who lived up the street from us. I enjoyed being with her and learning about spirituality, acceptance, empathy and the many different forms of generosity. This busy wife and mother of seven somehow found time for a highly sensitive, loving, clever and gifted little boy in great need of nurturing and encouragement. Her support was instrumental in helping me reach my full potential. We remained close for the remainder of her long and fruitful life.

Meeting Fernando Flores in January 1982 transformed my life as an adult. This Chilean born, world-renowned former politician granted me a full three-year scholarship to study ontology by his side. This opportunity, along with the works of ontological designer, Brian Regnier, eventually lead to my invention.

Later on, being a work at home father allowed me to enjoy every phase of both my sons' development to the fullest. Barrett and Spencer taught me much more than I could have ever taught them. They have become accomplished men and are in the midst of developing their own lives.

After a lifetime of searching, I found the right relationship and the right business partnership in my wife Carolyn. She empowers me ever so completely, in all aspects of life. She was able to fill that special hollow left when children grow up and move on. She is my brilliant, talented, artistic Princess Queen.

As a couple, we share the same aspirations and principles. We feel the same way about respect and dignity for others, especially in regard to children.

Spirituality had always been in my thoughts, but it was never clearer once Carolyn and I met. We are so well matched.

IN HER OWN WORDS...

Robert, it's thrilling to have finally met you in person. Though our paths may have crossed before in different ways, we had to wait patiently for the right time. With friends in common and living a mile apart for so long, provides great material for a whole other story. Being your wife and best friend is so fulfilling. I love you beyond words. Thank you for placing before me yet another artistic venue in which to be creative. Collaborating on this book series only proves how soulmates can be in communication without knowing. The focus of our work and our life philosophies blends so beautifully throughout these stories.

I give thanks to my beautiful (inside and out) talented mother and confidant for my connection to storytelling. Helene Silverman was an avid reader and prolific short story writer. She graduated high school at sixteen and eventually became an English and phonetics teacher to Latin American students in UT Austin. Soon after, she'd join the team that created English as a second language, known as ESL.

Watching her lead a life with unbounded love and ferocious loyalty towards her family and friends was invaluable. A passion for the arts, great sense of humor with perfectly timed sarcasm, innate talent for interior design and fashion, a fun sense of whimsy, an ability to write poems, song lyrics, short stories, and lists for any occasion; have all contributed to my own tapestry.

There's no doubt that she and Robert would have gotten along famously; they're alike in so many ways. At some level, he feels as if he knows her though they never met.

Attending art school at a young age provided a creative, imaginative, shy child, a voice with which to express myself freely. What I learned at such a young age influenced my decision to pursue my calling and my passion, interior design. After years in the industry, the process of remodeling and renovating opened my eyes to the high levels of stress imposed upon home and business owners. Lack of information and unexpected chaos caused much of their upset. I appreciate the numerous clients who continue trusting my intuition and follow a well thought out personalized process. Our work together is proof that this new spin on interior design is a thing of beauty and a healing art for children, teens and adults.

A Special Note...

Our desire, much like that of our characters, is to be understood and appreciated for who we are and for what we offer the world. In our case, it's being open-minded, imaginative and finding beauty all around.

As authors, we thrive by receiving enthusiastic feedback from our readers. We trust that you find Liberty 2041 Hexaseries fun, refreshing and enlightening.

Thank you, in advance, for sharing your impressions by writing a review on Amazon. We're excited you're joining our cause by finding your own ways of repairing the world.

For information on how Carolyn Gold, sensory interior designer and Robert Gold, trust development coach repair the world by transforming the lives of children, teens and adults, please visit:

thegoldtouch.net

LIBERTY WORLD

EXCLUSIVE

COMMUNICATION PLATFORM

UNITED WE STAND

FOR TRUST & UNITY

Interested in joining Jessica's initiative?

Great! Start by answering some questions:

1) What would you like to improve in the world right now?
2) Do you identify with any of Jessica's traits or her friends'?
3) Who's your favorite character— so far and why?
4) How should they handle life differently?
5) Are you an artist, author, fashionista, inventor or musician?
6) Do you see, smell, taste, hear or feel elements in our stories?
7) What are you eager to discover in upcoming episodes?
8) Comments & ideas?

We'd love to hear from you,

<u>libertyworld@liberty2041.com</u>

Write directly to Jessica and her friends and they'll respond.

Together we'll find ways to repair the world.

Robert & Carolyn Gold

LIBERTY 2041

Hexaseries

episode 1

Paperback & eBook

Short Reads

Perfectly perfect gifts for those

who like bite size adventures …

LIBERTY 2041

Hexaseries

episode 2
Paperback & eBook

Short Reads
Perfectly perfect gifts for those
who like bite size adventures …

www.ingramcontent.com/pod-product-compliance
Lightning Source LLC
Chambersburg PA
CBHW021247200726
48288CB00015B/2617